Time Travelling Through History

by F.J. Savina

Published by Research-publishing.net
Voillans, France; Dublin, Ireland
info@research-publishing.net

Time Travelling Through History
Written by F.J. Savina

The moral right of the author has been asserted

© 2012 by Research-publishing.net
Research-publishing.net is a not-for-profit association

Typeset by Research-publishing.net
Cover design: © Raphaël Savina (raphael@savina.net)
Illustrations: © Nicolas Fénix
Photo: © F.J. Savina (fj.savina@gmail.com)
Fonts used are licensed under a SIL Open Font License

ISBN13: 978-1-908416-02-5 (paperback)
Print on demand (lulu.com)

British Library Cataloguing-in-Publication Data.
A cataloguing record for this book is available from the British Library.

Bibliothèque Nationale de France - Dépôt légal: décembre 2012.

For history lovers

Contents

Foreword

Why should we be bothered with history? Reasons oft invoked are that history improves our judgment, provides us with an identity, or teaches us how to learn from others' mistakes. More importantly, it allows everyone to think for him or herself. For these reasons and more, history is a requisite for teaching subjects. It is concerned, of course, with what became of our ancestors, but it also relates to what happened this morning, which is already history!

As a part of her homeschooling, every two weeks, the author was given a time and place about which she had to research and write. Every time, she created a character who would have lived in those times. She could be a Roman baker in 177 A.D. enjoying the Gladiator games, or even a soldier under Genghis Khan in 1200 A.D. Over time, a background story of time travel developed, and the main character came into being. This unnamed individual would accidentally move through time as a disembodied soul, nesting itself into random people. This soul had to help itself or someone around it, before being able to move on to another person. It was the *sine qua non* for a safe return.

In order to accomplish these tales, the author firstly had to do extensive research in order to make them as historically accurate as possible. For each time travel, she learned dates, times, attires, and equally important, names. All she needed to accomplish these narratives was a little bit of imagination and access to the Internet. The main outcome was that she developed her critical thinking, improved her knowledge of history, and got her imagination and creativity running.

Now, begin your journey into various eras of this Earth through these romanticised, yet realistic chapters. Enjoy!

Sylvie Thouësny, Ph.D.

Prologue

Tina purred and rubbed her furry body against my legs. I gently shoved her away, and she stalked away in a mood. I needed to concentrate. One small drop. Just one. My face was so close to the conical beaker that condensation appeared on the glass surface with every short breath I took. My eyes were glued to the container I held carefully, tipping it inch by inch, waiting for that one drop to fall. I would have used my pipette, but it had broken the night before, and since it was the weekend, the school's lab was closed. I received minimal pocket money, and my busy schedule didn't allow for me to have a job. Buying a new one was not an immediate choice.

The beaker's bottom inched higher up, the yellow liquid inside moving, but no drop yet. This was crucial; it couldn't wait for the school pipette. This was the breakthrough of my life, the breakthrough of my seventeen year old life.

Just a little bit closer, a little bit closer, just a teeny bit more...

"BOO!!" my sister jumped out of nowhere and my surprise made me add two large drops of liquid. I froze, unsure what to do. These were unstable chemicals. My sister laughed and rolled on the floor, thinking she had sure got me this time. Moving only my head towards her, and keeping my arms frozen in midair, I screamed at her to get out. She realised I was serious and ran out crying, her voice mangled as she choked on tears. My head turned back to the conical beaker, its contents starting to bubble. I set down my arms carefully, and stepped back. I looked at my notes and realised that I may have owed my sister my future Nobel Prize. If my calculations were correct, this compound could break down molecules, and then put them back together again in a different time: time travelling.

I sat back in my plush chair, and thought of the scientific necessities. Before I could present my idea, I needed to create the 'antidote', the compound that brought the molecules back together. I set to work, and quite sometime later, I had my two bubbling liquids right beside one another, one yellow, one blue. Now, I only had to find a way to administer the liquid. I tried various methods on a plant, but everytime the thing just burned.

I went downstairs to the kitchen, and grabbed a piece of toast along with a ginger ale going back up to my bedroom filled with scientific apparel. Settling on my chair with my food, and chewing it slowly while staring at my creations, I didn't notice the ginger ale beside the two beakers, nor did I notice Tina who jumped up onto the table. I *did* notice, however, the ginger ale tipping over and spilling into both beakers as Tina missed her landing on the worktop. The startled cat, in her hurry out of the room, knocked over the two beakers. The toast fell out of my hand as I rushed forward to catch the beakers somehow. I fell short and the two beakers crashed onto the floor. There was an explosion.

My eyes were blinded with thick smoke and bright flashes. My mind was shocked, but it still functioned, and the scientist within me commented on what had probably happened, and what would probably happen next. The unstable chemicals, mixed with an unknown element in the ginger ale, created a reaction, and my body was disintegrating, while at the same time being exposed to the antidote.

I prepared myself for the possibility that I would end up in the past, or in the future. I only had time to see Tina's tail around the door before I felt myself disappearing...

2

Marie in the War

Marie Sklodowska was born in Warsaw, Poland, on the 7th of November, 1867. She died on July 4th 1934, in France, due to exposure to radioactive substances and pure radium for most of her life. Known as a great scientist who discovered two new elements (polonium, radium), she was also the first woman to receive a Nobel Prize, as well as the first person to receive two Nobels in a lifetime. At a young age, she moved to Paris where she became a governess to help her sister pay her college funds, who, when finished, returned the favor and aided Marie to pay the entrance fee for the Sorbonne. There she met Pierre Curie, a fellow student interested in science. They married and later had two daughters, Irene and Eve. Marie and Pierre joined forces and studied radioactivity, at which point they discovered radium. Pierre died on the rainy Thursday, 19th of April, 1906, in a road accident. Marie was devastated and became depressed. She sought companionship in her late husband's best friend, Paul Langevin. The media exposed their relationship and it practically destroyed her reputation and all she had achieved thus far. Additionally, since she was a woman, her achievements were seen as Pierre's achievements. When he died, she was expected to accept the government's offer of a pension to support herself and her children. She boldly refused and took her husband's job as a professor at the Sorbonne, and she continued her research. After the media outbreak, she fought hard to be respected again. When her second Nobel was given to her, she was cast in a new light. She then concentrated on finding the healing powers of radioactivity and she even travelled to battlefields during WWI to X-ray the wounded soldiers to locate bullet fragments in their bodies. She saved many lives.

I instantly jumped into her skin and I knew everything. I knew where and who I was from the memories in my newest brain. I sat up and looked around. The room was dark and gloomy, and in the distance I could hear the sudden bursts of canons being fired, and the distinct yet blurred sound of screaming and shouting filled the atmosphere with a morose feeling. I was lying on my hard bed, the bleached, white sheets scratching my legs. A woman in a nurse uniform was standing over me, and saying: "It's your shift."

I got up, scratched my still sleepy eyes and left the bed for my companion. I picked up the hat and hair pins from the bedside table and adjusted my white cap on my head. I quickly made my way through a white corridor, passing by doors which lead to great, big, white rooms full of injured people. Hurrying into this corridor, turning right there, left here, through there, and right again until I was finally in front of the door leading to my ward. I put on the white fabric filter over my mouth and nose and stepped into the living hell of our hospital. I tip-toed through the small spaces in between beds, checking each patient as I passed.

Jacques, a young boy of a soldier who had been standing too close to a hand grenade, was asleep in his bed. He was my main patient, although officially, everyone in the room was my patient. I was just more attached to Jacques. I sat by his bed and placed my hand on his forehead to check if he still had his fever. This woke him up, and he whispered in an exhausted voice.

"I'm feeling better now."

He smiled weakly as he attempted to say this. His face, distorted with bloody scars from the metal shrapnel implanted in his skin, was a sickly white and his eyes were watery and distant. He managed to smile without showing the pain of moving his facial muscles. I started his physical checkup and examined his many injuries. His arms had captured the biggest fragments of metal, and they had been removed without difficulty. I gently folded the covers up and gave a cry of shock as I saw his leg.

"Tell me the truth, is it bad?" Jacques didn't look at his leg, just straight up at the bright, white ceiling. I was horrified to see a great yellow and black bulge around the red line of a wound. It throbbed slightly, and small drops of dark, red blood and thick, yellow pus dripped out slowly, as if to show that each drop took him closer to death. I stared in horror at the comparison the gigantic, swollen leg made next to the almost normal, thin, white leg. Jacques made an audible gulp and turned his face away from me. I overcame my fears and turned back to Jacques' face. I looked at him with a look of determination in my eyes.

"I'm going to save you Jacques. I am going to keep trying, I'll try everything, I promise." Jacques turned to look at me and all he said was a 'thank you' in a soft, sad voice before falling into a troubled sleep. I started to clean his facial wounds first, to avoid having another infection to take care of. I got my tweezers and started extracting the pieces of metal in from face. He kept his eyes closed and winced from time to time, but otherwise, he never manisfested his pain. I cleaned up his face with warm water, delicately bandaging it, leaving holes around his eyes, nose and mouth. Moving downwards to his neck, torso, and arms, his body slowly became engulfed in bandages. His chest had been relatively undamaged because of the layers he had been wearing. By the time I had finished bandaging and cleaning all his wounds, it was already late, and I knew I had other patients to attend to. Hesitating for just a moment, I went against hospital rules and ignored the other patients, who could all wait until morning. I replaced the dirty water and slowly washed away the cracked, dry blood on Jacques' calf.

At the slightest pressure, he winced and moaned, more pus dripping out. Eventually, a voice called out saying 'Lights out!' and I said goodnight to Jacques. I made my way back towards my so-called 'bed' and found the other nurses talking, most likely about the usual gossip.

"Yes, and did I tell you about that man who got that girl pregnant?"

"Oh, no! He didn't!"

"Yes, he did! And he refused to marry her! Can you believe it?"

I got into my bed but found I couldn't sleep. I listened to the chatter of the other nurses instead, hoping their voices would lull me to sleep.

"Did you you hear what the doctors announced?"

"No, what did they say?"

"Marie Curie is coming to our hospital to set up her radiological instrument."

"*The* Marie Curie?"

"Yes, and she is going to show all of us how to use the X-rays. With such an invention we could note the location of every bit of metal in a patient's body."

"If you don't break the machine first!" laughed one nurse. The other nurses laughed along with her, and the conversation moved back to the latest relationship gossip.

The idea was so dream-like. I liked it. In this dream I could save Jacques, I could find the pieces of metal that were infecting his leg. I could...I could...

~~~

I woke up and found that there was no one in the dorm. How could I have slept in? Why did no one wake me? I glanced up at the clock; it was four in the morning. I was not too late. But where was everyone? Hearing distinct chatter coming from the court outside, I got up, not even bothering to tie my hair or put on my hat. I ran and ran down the corridors, until from a window I saw a grey, flat-nosed Renault. It had a cross and the French flag painted on the sides.

The doctors and nurses were all heading back inside, anticipation on their faces. I continued down the hallway and arrived at the back of a crowd. Through the mass of nurses and doctors I saw a woman with her hair tied up in a bun. She was dressed in a dark grey dress and was carrying an old yellow, worn leather bag, which was slung carelessly over her shoulder. She was talking to the head of the hospital as he was directing her throughout the corridors. She was lead into one of our storerooms which, as I saw later, had been transformed into a makeshift laboratory. There were great, big, metal cases and tiny, fragile glass tubes in one corner, as well as a hospital bed on the opposite end. The room was quite spacious and at least four wounded soldiers could be accommodated with ease.

I suddenly realised I hadn't dreamt the coming of Marie Curie. Excitement flushed over me, but it was quickly subdued by anger. Just because she was famous, had two Nobels and was considered a genius, she was given a bigger, cozier and better room than the people who actually worked around here. I stormed out of the crowd, furious with her luxury, and I went to get my hat. I knew deep down that I was wrong, but my pride silenced that small voice of conscience. I tied my hair, adjusted my hat and apron on the way to attend to Jacques and was devastated to see that his leg had not gotten better. In fact, it had gotten worse, much worse. It was constantly bleeding, the blood flowing down thick and black. Jacques' breathing was heavy and irregular, and the entire leg had swollen to a large, dark yellowish bulge. My hand covered my mouth and I stifled a small little shriek.

Jacques looked up at the sound and he went pale when he saw my face. He started to turn his head from side to side, and his hands reached out to grab me. His motion brought him upwards, but he became still when he saw his leg. Suddenly, he turned to the bucket on the side of the bed, already full from his neighbour's stomach fits, and retched. It didn't last long, as he didn't have much in his stomach to begin with. He looked up from the bucket and begged me not to take his leg, while also begging me to make the hurt stop. He got into hysterics and I was forced to calm him down, giving him a shot of morphine. He fell into a forced, troubled sleep and I left him to go ask the doctor what could be done. The doctor, I found out, was with Marie Curie. I marched down the corridor and bumped into a nurse coming the other way. She was followed by two helpers carrying a soldier.

"Another death?" I asked. She smiled, which surprised me, and she exclaimed:

"Goodness no! He is going to live now that the bullet in his liver has been removed! It is Marie Curie! She can see straight through the flesh and detect the bullet. I am fetching another patient!" The nurse ran off while she said that last phrase. I moved forward in a hurry, and saw a great line of wounded soldiers, leading up to the door which I had thought led to Marie's room. I felt ashamed for not listening to my heart and thinking bad things of Marie Curie. Jacques could be scanned and then the metal that was killing him could be extracted. I hurried the opposite way I had come with a stretcher and its two carriers I had grabbed on the way, and with their help, I moved Jacques. He cried out in pain regardless of his drugged stupor. The stretcher and I arrived at the hallway to the door, and only then did I truly see how long the queue was. Did we really have hundreds of soldiers in need of this new technology? My eyes watered when I heard Jacques whimper.

The hours drained by endlessly. It came to the point where I had to leave Jacques alone in the line to attend to others. The day went by and Jacques was close to his turn. On one of my hourly check-ups on him, I had the chance of arriving just as he was being ushered into what had been nicknamed the Radiation Room.

Professional hands took Jacques from the stretcher and settled him under this big, black 'spider leg', for lack of a better description. It extended over him and was dragged down over his body. There were trays and liquids everywhere, and the room was very dark; there were thick, black blankets hung over the windows. Marie Curie did some things over here, and some things over there, and eventually she presented a picture of Jacques' leg. Well, a picture of his skeletal leg. There were white spots on the image as well. The image was placed in a file for Jacques, and the stretcher was then brought to the operating room. Before the stretcher had even left, the bed under the 'spider' was already occupied with a new soldier.

In the operating room, the doctor used the image as a reference while he prodded around in Jacques' wound. The surgical tweezers twisted and turned in Jacques' gaping wound, and pus that I thought had been removed squirted out. The foreign object moving around caused the wound to bleed even harder. I held my breath, and when I started seeing shapes, I realised I wasn't breathing, and took in a quick short breath.

The doctor kept extracting shrapnel after shrapnel, some smaller than needles. The morphine shot had worn off hours ago, but seeing the state of Jacques' leg, the doctor had allowed for another shot for the operation.

Eventually, the bits of metal were accounted for, and thanking the doctor, I escorted Jacques out of the room. Once back in his spot, the stretcher went off to another nurse. I got to work on extracting the remaining pus and stopping the blood. I sang him a lullaby as I worked, although I wasn't sure if with the morphine if he could hear me. Bandage after bandage, I grew certain that he would live, and perhaps, even walk.

"Live and walk, Jacques." I smiled at him.

~~~

I sipped my tea, enjoying the scarce sunlight on my face. I watched as Jacques walked around and around in the courtyard with his walking stick. He constantly waved and smiled back at me, and I constantly had to wave and smile back. I got up from the bench I was sitting on and called out to him. He came walking back, frowning and whining when I told him it was getting dark and that we should get back into the hospital. He obliged anyway and followed me back into the building. My pace however, was too slow, so he ran ahead and I was left to trail behind him. Still, when he reached the door, he looked back and waved again.

My head ached and I felt suddenly dizzy. The dull grey of the courtyard around me turned and turned and it dissolved into brighter colours, spiraling out. I felt tugged and the colours called out to me, beckoning me to them. I was sucked in and I was falling yet floating at the same time. Where will I go now?

3

The Prince

*M*artin Luther was born on the 10th of November, 1483, and died on the 18th of February, 1546. He was a German priest, and later a professor of theology. He initiated the Protestant Reformation with a list of 95 points he believed were wrong with the church. He pegged this list, called the 95 Theses, to the door of a church in his village so everyone could see and read it. At that time, the church was very powerful and the pope was the one everyone looked up to. The church offered 'indulgences', meaning that you could buy your way into heaven, or obtain less years in purgatory. Luther was against this idea, and believed that it was your faith that gave you access to heaven, not your money. The pope was not happy; his income was decreasing steadily as more and more people sided with Luther's beliefs. At first, the Pope asked Luther to reject his claims, or he would be excommunicated for heresy. When Luther did not repent, the pope sent a Papal Bull, an official document asking him to repent. Luther used it along with other paper indulgences the villagers had as a starting ignition for a public barbecue. He was then called to Worms by Charles V, the Holy Roman Emperor, for a trial. He was promised safe passage and when asked to repent all his works and writings as heresy, he refused. He said he saw no fault, and could not be convinced that there was any unless it was proven by the Scriptures (bible). He was excommunicated and declared a criminal. However, on his way home, he was kidnapped by his friend, Frederick III, Elector of Saxony, who wanted to keep Luther safe. Luther stayed in hiding for a year, during which time he translated the Bible from Latin to German. He later married a runaway nun named Katharina von Bora. Luther decided that the only way to reform the church would be to fight, and he convinced many leaders to convert to Protestantism. These princes formed an alliance called the Schmalkaldic League, who would later start a religion war with the Christians.

I instantly jumped into his skin and I knew everything. I knew where and who I was from the memories in my newest brain. I walked up the steps towards the church door, with my servants following behind me. The peasants of my little town bowed down to me and let me pass. I stepped into the church and took my place in the front, settling comfortably in my cushioned chair. The big gothic church was filling up fast with all sorts of people. The church bell rang out to indicate the start of the mass. Everyone was silent, except for the choir of boys singing a holy song. They finished the song five minutes later, and I knew we weren't going to have our mass yet again this Sunday. The peasants stayed silent, while the nobles and I discussed what we should do. Deciding that we would all pray for the normal duration of a mass, I set myself to the task of personally sorting out this problem. I said my Hail Marys and asked for forgiveness. The bells rang again and everyone exited the church, nobles first of course. I entered my carriage at the bottom of the church steps and as I was being driven back to my home, I thought of the weight of my responsibilities and my problems. We were in the middle of a war, although it was soon to be over. The Empire was being attacked from all sides, and now it was breaking from within. This Martin Luther fellow was creating havoc. As treacherous as he was, and even if he did cause unnecessary problems, I did see his point; I could not let my people live without their mass. The church needed to control and discipline its priests and monks. Our priest had been given his role at the age of twelve by his uncle, a cardinal. Now, he had bought more positions in other parishes, although he could not be in two places at once.

I had once found out he had three priest licenses, and was 'saving up' to be a bishop. On the very rare occasions that he did appear for our mass, he was often late and services were always the same. Although I knew some prayers in Latin, I could not read the Holy Gospels. Even so, there was something about the way our priest read from the Bible. It was as if he just couldn't speak the Holy language, stuttering it out instead.

I supposed he had not undergone all his theology classes before becoming a priest. After all, he had barely reached marrying age when he was declared a messenger of God! I agreed with this Luther, the church needed to be reminded of its place.

Feeling the carriage stop, I waited for the door to be opened. I stepped out and walked up the steps of my homestead. My servants opened doors that stood in my way, and as I passed the door to the kitchen, I asked for a breakfast to be delivered into my study. I finally reached my destination, the study, and settled into the big, ornamented, plush, leather chair.

I took out my plume pen from Paris and a sheet of heavy, expensive paper. I wanted to be a part of this, whatever 'this' was. If it was a war, then so be it.

I inscribed onto the sheet my concerns in a letter for Philip of Hesse, proclaimed a great Protestant Leader. Thinking back, the reformation had started long ago, but I felt my help was needed in order to give it a boost.

Once my letter was done, I signed and enclosed it in an envelope. Ringing my little bell, a messenger came to take it away and deliver it. I had always had modest views of myself, but I knew my involvement would be a great advantage. While waiting for my breakfast, I lounged around in my study, daydreaming. Eventually, a splendid roasted duck with apple sauce was delivered. My mouth watered at the smell and look of it.

Having stuffed myself, I went to bed for nap, as per usual, but I could not exactly fall asleep; too many things were going on inside my head. Had the messenger delivered the letter? Would Philip of Hesse accept my proposition? I thought of the letter I had sent, rethinking through its contents. I had recently learned that a league of Protestant Rulers was being formed. I had read this in a paper.

Apparently, Philip of Hesse was one of the founding rulers. Thinking of almost half my taxe incomes going to the pope made my blood boil. It wasn't as if the Church, or the pope, actually used it charitably. Enough was enough.

I turned around on the bed, fluffed my overly large pillows and tried to find a comfortable position. I gave up searching, and lighting a candle, I reached for a book on my bedside table. The words made no sense on the paper. I put the book away, but did not put out the candle. I stayed in bed, thinking of the new league. What a name; the Schmalkaldic League! It was formed of an alliance, each vowing to protect one another from any religious or political attacks. How nice that must be. It was a good way of saying to the world that I wanted change.

Both my village and I would benefit from it. We would actually get our daily masses and confessions. We, I, would be immediately richer, since I wouldn't have to keep paying for indulgences, although it also meant I had to pray more, and work harder to earn my place in heaven...

The candle had not been a very big one, and the light was already dimming. I settled back down and waited for the candle to die of its own accord.

~~~

Several weeks later, I was awoken from a night's sleep by a servant.

"Did your Highness sleep well?" asked the girl while she was bringing up a big platter of assorted breads and cheeses.

"No!" I cried out in a grumpy, almost childish manner. My night had been spent tossing and turning. I had hardly slept at all. Why hadn't I received an answer from Philips yet? Had the messenger stopped at a brewery? Gotten lost? Mugged?!

I picked up my knife roughly and ate without any appetite. I had hardly eaten half when the messenger was announced by the porter.

I immediately forgot my crankiness, being too preoccupied with the letter. I pushed my platter to the side and got up. I hastily took the letter opener from a small desk, and ripped open the rough paper. I scanned through it while wondering what it would contain. Thinking in such a way prevented me from understanding the words, so I tried again, slowly,

23

meticulously. My room attendants were all looking at their feet, but I knew they were just as excited and interested as I was. Thus, I read aloud the main points of the letter.

"Dear..., We have discussed your proposition as founders of the Schmalkaldic League... come to the conclusion that you are accepted as a viable asset to our organisation against the Catholic church!" My joy was so great I almost screamed out the last part. The servants too took the liberty of jumping in the air with joy. I was so happy I forgot our class differences, and told my favorite attendant, Matthew, to prepare a big festival to which the entire village would be invited. I spent the next hour going over party details. I finally went back to my study alone, letter clutched tightly in hand, and I realised I had forgotten to read its entirety. I read through it and slightly lost my enthusiasm, although only slightly. I rang for and said to my faithful Matthew,

"Matthew?"

"Yes, Sir?" enquired the young man.

"It seems I have to attend a meeting next week in order to become an official member, or at least to be considered as such. Maybe we should wait until after that to have this party."

"Yes, Sir. That seems to be the best solution."

I waved my hand in dismissal, and Matthew was gone in seconds. It was only then I realised I wasn't dressed. By myself, I hadn't managed to get all the layers to align properly, but I believed I looked respectable.

Sitting down at my desk, I procured myself a sheet of paper and a newly made quill. I kindly replied to Philip of Hesse's letter, highlighting the gratitude and relief I felt.

Once the little note was finished, I called my messenger back in, along with several room attendants. I addressed the messenger,

"Boy, deliver this letter to Philip of Hesse. I do not expect a reply."

"Yes, Your Highness."

"Sir, might I dare to bring something to your attention?" asked Matthew.

"Yes, yes, go ahead, dare." I waved my hand at him as I talked, as a way of encouraging speech.

"Your Highness seems to have put his clothing on backward. Sir." Matthew added a hesitant 'sir' at the end, not sure if his statement would aggravate me or not.

"Oh my! It seems I have! Come help me." Matthew and the attendants crossed the room towards me, slipping me out of my clothes. As I was in my undergarments, and waiting for the first clothes to be slipped over my head, I noticed a smell in the room.

"By God! What is that pungent smell?" I looked around as if I could see where it originated from. The servants gave each other nervous glances. Matthew said slowly and hesitatingly:

"Your Highness has not bathed in several months... perhaps that might be the cause. Your Highness." Matthew flinched, but no anger came from me. I simply answered back,

"Well, that would account for why the smell has been worse and worse everyday! Haha!" The servants laughed along nervously.

"Perhaps it is best I take a bath the day before the meeting." I nodded to myself, my sentence being more of a statement than a suggestion. As I laughed jovially, I thought of all the plans and budgets that had to be made and reassessed. The theatre I had always wanted in my town would finally be able to be constructed.

~~~

The week droned by, plans for my villa to be restored and leaking roofs to be rebuilt were made. Our town would thrive much more than it had before, trapped in the claws of the pope. Before I realised it, it was the day before the meeting, and as arranged, I took a hot bath. I basked in the water, while my maids scrubbed soap into my skin in an effort to rub away the grime.

Tomorrow would be a day to be remembered. The thought brought a smile to my face.

The steam and white sheets in my bathroom turned and turned around me and they dissolved into brighter colours, spiraling out. I felt tugged and the reds and blues and yellows called out to me, beckoning me to them. I was sucked in and I was falling yet floating at the same time. Where will I go now?

4

Kitty's Fight

Emmeline Goulden was born in Manchester in 1858 and she died on the 14th of July, 1928. She died shortly after the voting rights for women were lowered to the same age as men. She grew up in a politically active family, which may quite possibly be the reason she entered into women's suffrage. She married Richard Pankhurst, a plublic supporter of women's suffrage. When he died of a gastric ulcer in 1898, Emmeline was in shock, but regardless, she threw herself completely into women's suffrage. She formed a group named the Women's Franchise League. The group gave speeches and announcements, but Emmeline found that the government did not really care. She decided to win the women's vote in a different way. She formed a new group, which was to revolutionise the fight for women's rights. The group was called the Women's Social and Political Union (WSPU). It was a militant group, using destruction and violence to get the attention of the public and the government. It was the WSPU that came up with the term 'Suffragette'. Emmeline led the group of women, all willing to be jailed repeatedly for smashing windows and disturbing the 'peace'. The government was surprised that it had to imprison and fine these women, and that once they were released they would have to be imprisoned and fined yet again. This was known as the Cat and Mouse Act. Their protest got to the point where they would starve themselves in prison, and as a result, they were forced-fed with tubes inserted into their throats by 'qualified doctors'. However, when WWI broke out, and England declared war on Germany, Emmeline completely changed her political priorities.

I instantly jumped into her skin and I knew everything. I knew where and who I was from the memories in my newest brain. Walking down the busy Nelson Street, I turned to face one of the houses. My hand stopped over the knocker. Taking a deep breath and holding it for a moment, I finally let out all the air. My hand brought the knocker up and then slammed it down three times. A tall, slender woman with greying hair harshly opened the door, and looked me up and down. A prettier young girl, with her mother's severe face, appeared in the doorway.

"Hello, Kitty."

"Hello, Emmeline." I replied. Our greetings had a great sense of formality, both of us standing tall, me outside the doorway, her with her hand still holding the door open.

"Well, do come on in." Emmeline stepped to the side with her severe-faced daughter doing the same. That sense of formality was still there, and I kept my back straight and my voice even as I uttered a thank you. Emmeline Pankhurst turned her back to me and led me into an austere living room. Christabel, the daughter, stayed behind me, and I felt like a prisoner being led into a cell, one guard in front and one behind. The bang of the front door being closed hadn't helped me fight my sense of entrapment. I quickly imagined making a run for it, but my plans were interrupted by a voice in my head, 'think of all the women who live in the shadows of men', it said.

I shook my head. I had to continue my mission, there was no space for failure. Accepting a cup of tea, I settled on one of the flowered chairs. There were a few embers in the fireplace beside me, and as I looked at them, trying to muster up the courage to say what was on my mind, Emmeline started a conversation. It was not very interesting, something about an embroidery class. While interrupting and relishing the look on her face at the interruption, I stated my true intentions for the visit.

"Emmeline, we have to talk."

"I thought we already were." She had a nasty tone which made my anger boil up.

"I heard you signed a contract with the government."

"I did." Emmeline replied.

Her calmness and full approval of this fact angered me even more. I let it all fly out.

"Have you lost your mind?! This is the moment when the government is the weakest, if we keep demanding the women's suffrage, if we keep fighting for the right to vote, they will grant it just to make us one less problem, but after the war, it'll be too late for them to realise what they have done. We could finally have the vote!" My hands moved up and down as if they were describing what I was saying. Emmeline's eyes were starting to squint, and I could tell she would not be merciful in her rebuke.

"Kitty, I see your ideas about the aims of this group are muddled. The way I see it, you are demanding we continue to annoy the government, and prevent them from winning this war. You are a pro-German, and you are forthwith banned from this group." She resembled a judge as she told me what my fate would be, all that was missing was a gavel and a great big white wig. I sat motionless for a while. I couldn't believe what she was saying. She was accusing me of being for the war, for the Germans! I set down my untouched cup of tea and stood up. Emmeline was still sitting as straight as ever, with only her eyes moving up with me. I exclaimed:

"You are a very mean woman. Someday, someone will recognise that and that person will stand up to you! You fascist! I am not banned! I am leaving this horrible group! And I might take some others with me!"

I turned my back to her, and moved towards the front door.

"I'll show myself out." I never glanced back at Emmeline nor her daughter. That was the last time I ever saw them, but not the last time I ever heard of or talked about them.

I walked in the streets towards my home, thinking of my available options. I could start a new group of women – and men – who were still willing to fight for the right to vote. But would I find enough of those willing people? As soon as England had declared war, it seemed that the British people were split up into two categories: pacifists and antagonists. I hoped there were some in between, like me. I was not for the war, it was a violent and savage thing which should no longer be accepted in our civilised time. However, I still saw the usefulness of such a war; why not use it to our advantage? By continually demanding the vote for women, surely the easiest thing for the government to do was to give us said vote, then, they could concentrate solely on the war. Unfortunately, Emmeline did not share my point of view. In fact, her opinion was constantly changing.

There was a time when I had admired her; she had fought for women's freedom, quite literally. She had started the militant movement, and she was so devoted. But she had changed radically. She had even went as far as buying a one-way ticket to Australia for one of her daughters because said daughter hadn't shared the same ideas as her mother.

And now, she had banned me from the group, although I wasn't the first person to be banned. Almost in secret, she had made a contract with the government without consulting any of the affected members of the group.

I reached my house and made myself a cup of tea,

settling on my sofa in the small living room. I sat still and listened to the grandfather's clock in my hallway tick-tocking away. The soothing, regular sounds helped me reach my resolution.

Again, I set down an untouched cup of tea, and grabbing my coat and hat, put them on before heading out the door. I went into the street and half ran to my friend's house. She had a telephone, and once there I used it to phone a list of members I knew, asking all of them to meet at my house for an emergency meeting concerning the entire group. I asked Anna, the friend with the phone, personally if she would come too. She agreed, but it was obvious she was confused.

We both hurried back to my home, in fear of someone arriving before us, but no one was waiting on the porch when we arrived. She helped me put some biscuits out and made a new batch of tea.

This time, I really would drink it, I told myself. Just as the preparation of the round table in the dining room was finished, the first of our 'guests' arrived.

After ten minutes, the table was filled up, the biscuits partly eaten, the tea sipped, and my speech started.

"Ladies, some of you may know why I have called you here, and some of you may not."

"Where's Emmeline? Is this not a formal meeting?" asked a women with a pink hat on. Cathy, she was called.

"Cathy, you know Emmeline 'banned' meetings a while ago. In fact, this is touching on the subject for which I have brought you all here. Emmeline Pankhurst." All the women at the table gave somewhat of a murmur and looked about at each other. I continued:

"I believe she has lost her belief in women's suffrage. I... I also think she has become a fascist." Helen exclaimed out at my last statement.

"That is preposterous! Emmeline is a great lady!" Helen was a rather plump woman giving in to her forties. She was dressed in a yellow dress, with a lime green hat propped sideways on her head. Countering her with a rhetorical question:

"Why do you think she stopped having weekly meetings since that girl proposed a change in our ways of winning over the vote?" I nodded slightly as I said this. Helen merely looked down at the table, gulped, and her cheeks reddened a little. I resumed my speech.

"I have called you all here because I am unhappy with Emmeline. Today, she banned me from the group. Officially, I am no longer an existing member of the WSPU. I was banned because I said what I thought. I was immediately proclaimed a pro-German, and that was that. We all know this isn't the first person to be excluded for speaking their mind. So yes, Helen, I do believe Emmeline has become a fascist, an antagonist, and her priorities are no longer in accordance to what this group was founded for in the first place. So I am asking all of you, are you going to hide in the shadow of this woman as she does things in your name, things you may not agree with? I will not, and that is why I am forming a new group, a feminist group, who isn't all for the war, but profits from it by probing the government to give us the vote." I had spoken almost without inhaling, and by the end, I was breathing hard, trying to catch my breath. A lady with whom I was not exactly familiar with asked in a confused voice:

"But, what had you said to result in your ban, and are we not already using this ridiculous war to our advantage?" She was frowning slightly, and worry lines appeared on her forehead as she did so. My expressions soon turned to shock as I realised she had no idea of the contract Emmeline had signed. Of course, how silly of me... Emmeline had not discussed it, she had simply signed it for us!

"I... I assumed everyone had been informed. Emmeline signed a contract with the government. It is now apparent not only did she not consult any of us, but she also kept it secret from the majority of you. The only soul Emmeline probably did tell was Christabel, her ever faithful *servant*."

When some of the women frowned in confusion, I explained:

"Christabel being Emmeline's daughter, she is either afraid of her mother, which I think, most of us are, or she was brainwashed by her. Christabel has always agreed with Emmeline; she is the only daughter who ever has. As for the contract, well... it is good, but also very bad. Briefly, it states that all the women from the W.S.P.U. who are in prison will be released, on the condition that Emmeline stop being a militant. These are hard times, after all. I know what most of you are thinking, 'that isn't a bad thing, anyone with common sense wouldn't fight with the government while it was in a bigger fight that if lost would mean great change in England', but Emmeline has also signed on to advertise the war. She has actually agreed to encourage young men to go be killed, and she is probably changing the title of our newspaper as we speak. Her patriotism is worthy of admiration, but you must admit it is suspicious, especially considering not three months ago she went about declaring how ignorant the government was in all their male glory!"

The women stayed silent, so I sprung on,

"I say stand up to Emmeline, and fight for what you believe in. Who is with me?" I looked around and felt a little breathless as I looked around the table at the women. I felt my heart drop as I started to realise I was the only one here with sense, but it was soon uplifted when at least half of the women started clapping and nodding in approval. The ones who weren't in approval, slowly stood up, and walked out without any warnings. Only Helen, who was apparently still in admiration of Emmeline, said in a progressively menacing voice:

"I am sorry you think that way, Kitty Marion. But tell me, are you not German born?" I was surprised she knew this, and my head reeled back in surprise.

"And so what if I am? I came here to fight for the women who couldn't, and that's what I intend to do." My tone was defensive, and Helen took it as an invitation to get up and walk towards me, saying in a matter-of-fact way:

"Doesn't everyone have a sense of patriotism to their country of birth?" She faced me full on now; all the women who were still there followed the conversation with darting eyes and silent mouths. I met Helen halfway so that it resulted with us nose-to-nose.

"I am neither for the Germans, nor for the English." This confused Helen. I took pleasure in her muddled state.

"You could say I am a pacifist of some kind; I do not encourage war, but if it does perchance happen, no matter who is fighting who, I will see the profit to be made for the people, and I will take advantage of that profit."

Helen, still confused and even more muddled, turned round and stalked out of the room.

The remaining women gave me a polite clapping, and we all said good bye, agreeing to see Emmeline tomorrow to tell her we were unhappy and that we were leaving.

It was obvious my reputation here had been ruined; at the moment, no one in England was fond of Germans in general. Perhaps I could to America to start my new political life. If I could not help here, I would help elsewhere.

Everyone gone, I left the mess on the table as it was and crawled under the covers of my bed. Feeling safe and warm, I thought about all the great things I would be able to do for women without having Emmeline breathing down my neck.

The floral wallpaper of my room around me turned and turned and it dissolved into brighter colours, spiraling out. I felt tugged and the reds and blues and yellows called out to me, beckoning them to me. I was sucked in and I was falling yet floating at the same time. Where will I go now?

5

Temüjin and Börte

*G*enghis Khan, born as Temüjin, was the founder and ruler of the Mongol Empire, the largest contiguous empire in history. He came to power by uniting the many nomadic tribes situated in northeast Asia. While nine years old, he was brought by his father to pick his bride. While stopped at a village to rest, little Temüjin chose young Börte and promised her he would come back in five years when he was at the marriageable age. While this angered Temüjin's father at first, he saw how determined his son was, and caved in on his demand. On the way back from the neighboring tribe, the party stopped at a traditional resting spot and found themselves eating alongside one of their common enemies. Temüjin's father, Yesügei, followed the Mongolian tradition and exchanged food with the tribe. Although he greatly suspected the others' food to be poisoned, he ate anyway and died. Temüjin was still too young to rule the Borjigin (tribe), and the Khan's advisors took the oppurtunity to enrich themselves by stealing

*from their leader. They badly wanted to kill Temüjin,
but according to tradition, it was forbidden to kill
children. He was to be kept prisoner and fed until he
surpassed the wheel of a cart, which meant he was
then no longer a child. Temüjin, aware of his fate,
escaped but was recaptured, only to escape again.
Once he was free yet again, he finally went to collect
his bride, Börte, only to lose her to the Merkits, an
enemy clan of Temüjin's late father.*

I instantly jumped into his skin and I knew
everything. I knew where and who I was from the
memories in my newest brain. I took the wooden
bowl from the soldier beside me and settled myself
more comfortably around the blazing fire.

It was a rather chilly night and a wolf howled in the
distance, although it was practically drowned out
by the low-pitched singing of the drunk soldiers
around the burning wood. My fingers curled around
the bowl, and not being able to ignore my stomach
any longer, I dug into the soup. I always drank the
watery part of the 'soup' first, eating the tasty meat
last.

One of the soldiers from my Arav had hunted down
a rabbit who had unfortunately scurried home,
taking the hunter to a burrow of several rabbits. He

had also spotted a squirrel. Regrettably, we all had to give our finds to Jamuka, our Khan, however, we always kept some for ourselves. This time we kept two rabbits and the robust squirrel.

It was a relief to end my hunger. I wiped my greasy fingers on the damp grass and stretched out my stiff legs from the long journey on horseback. Tomorrow we were to fight, and I needed my strength. I crossed my legs back underneath me and picked up a bowl of milk. This was very fine; the mare must have been a vigorous filly. Whoever had fermented the milk had done a very good job, anyway.

A hand slapped me on the back and I felt the milk slither down the wrong pipe and enter into my lungs. I coughed and spluttered. The liquid came back up, and I spat it out onto the fire, which flickered angrily at the sudden attack. Nekhii laughed at me and let himself drop down heavily on the grass beside me. He let out an 'OOF' as he dropped, as well as a loud belch. He was obviously drunk.

"Hey! How are you?" he shouted into my ear. Nekhii was a 'friend' from my Arav. There were ten of us and we were one of the ten Aravs that made up a Zuut. He was always cheery and very optimistic. He also had a knack for trouble, fighting and drinking.

Nekhii leaned in very closely to me and squinted his eyes. After a while he leaned back and shouted:

"Hey! Do you know why we're off fighting the Merkits?"

"No, but you're going to tell me, aren't you?" I rolled my eyes.

"How did you know?" He looked at me seriously as he said this. He was easily sidetracked, but he soon came back to his excitement of knowing something I didn't.

"Well, I heard from this guy who had heard from his brother who overhead Jamuka and Temüjin talking, way back at home. Well actually, I think it was the brother who heard from the guy and the brother told me, or is it the other way round?" He starting muttering to himself and tracing patterns in the air with his greasy fingers, going from one imaginary person to the other. This continued until I broke his trance:

"What did you hear?!"

Nekhii stared at me and finally said,

"Oh yeah, yeah. Right. Well, Jamuka, our, you know, Khan, tribe leader person..."

I cut him off.

"I know who Jamuka is. Just get to the point."

He continued.

"Well, you know the way to be a proper Mongol, you have to be on horseback, or own a horse, be married, stuff like that." I thought of my horse, Batkha number six and my two other "just in case horses", Batkha seven and Batkha eight. This reminded me, I had forgotten to feed them. Oh well, they would find something to graze. My mind jumped to my wives. I hoped they would be smart enough to cook my favorite meat when I returned. I turned back to Nekhii and nodded.

"You also have to have a blood brother. Hey, do you know how you become someone's blood brother? Do you?" My mind wandered to when I was ten. Tömör and I were best friends, so we decided to be blood brothers. I shook my head with annoyance.

"Of course I know how to become a blood brother. Get to the point. What do you want to tell me?!"

Nekhii continued without paying attention to what I was saying.

"Well, it's basically when you cut your hand, and you let a couple of drops fall into a bowl of milk. Then the other guy does the same and lets the drops fall in the same bowl, and then the two of them take a sip each. Apparently, Jamuka and Temüjin are blood brothers. And Temüjin is married to a girl called Börte. Hold on. Let's start from the beginning. Temüjin's father went on a raid in the Merkit territory. He stole a beautiful woman although she was already the bride of the tribe leader. Nevertheless, she was married to Yesügei anyway. The Merkits swore that they would get revenge. Later on, once Temüjin was nine years old, he was supposed to marry a Merkit girl to ensure the much needed peace." Nekhii took a sip of his own bowl of milk, looked at the fire and then continued.

"So Yesügei took his son to the Merkit tribe, but they stopped at a smaller tribe on the way there and decided to spend the night. Temüjin, the sly little devil, tricked his father, and the little rascal chose a bride there; Börte. Then you know the rest, his father died, and he was replaced by Targutai, the Khan's advisor. He stole everything from Temüjin and left him and his family to rot in poverty without a tribe, you get the drift. After Temüjin escaped for the second time from Targutai, he decided to fetch his wife. They got married, and he brought her back to his mother." My head stooped and my eyes were closing very slowly. The moon was very high up in the sky. Nekhii's voice had become white noise in the background, joining the howls of the wolves.

"THEN!" I jumped up as he shouted to emphasize

that he had advanced in his story. I tried to pay attention and keep my eyes open.

"Then! The Merkits heard that Temüjin got married, and they thought this was the perfect opportunity for revenge. They kidnapped Börte, and she was to be wed to the dude that had lost his wife to Yesügei." Nekhii's arms, in a quick jerky movement, gave himself a hug, representing the kidnapping.

"Temüjin asked our Khan and his father's old blood brother for help to make war with the Merkits. And thus, we are fighting for a woman!" he cried out triumphantly.

My sleepiness went away in an instant.

"But we don't go to war over women! It is not the Mongol way!" I was shocked that this one man had gotten upset over a woman! Surely, at the snap of a finger, he could have two more beautiful women instantly.

I watched Nekhii return to wherever it was he had come from in the first place. He was most likely going to find someone else to tell his story to. I curled up in my bed of furs simply placed on the ground.

~~~

The next morning I was awakened with a kick in the gut.

"Get up! We have Merkits to fight!" While groaning,

I got up and replaced my fur hat onto my numb ears. Once the camp cleared out, I attended to my horses. I prepared them and got my sword and bow and arrows. We made our way to the rocky Merkit territory, towards the village which held Börte.

Suddenly, we were ambushed by hidden enemies. Their frightening masks must have caused several soldiers to freeze in fear, with their fur faces, slits as eyes. They weren't on horseback but could jump from rock to rock to attack you. My arms went on automatic as I aimed for everything with a mask. The world seemed to work in slow motion, yet everything zoomed by. My mouth opened itself and a yell came out.

I was suddenly falling, and I crashed into the hard ground, avoiding the rocks by an inch. My horse, that great big carcass, fell on top of me and knocked the air out of me. I was hidden from the enemies yet I was suffocating under the horse's weight. Blood, sweet and rusty, trickled from the horse's side, down his back and onto my forehead, dripping to my chin. As suddenly as it began, the fighting ended; everything was silent. The sound of a sword digging into flesh resonated for the last time, and victory was sweet in the air. I tried shoving Batkha off, crying for help as I did so.

Nekhii came rushing up with blood on his arm and a missing hat. With his help I managed to be set free. I looked around at the battlefield, and at the littered corpses.

In the distance, a man was stepping over the rocks and bodies as he guided a woman forwards. A servant ran up to Temüjin and gave him a horse he had found. Temüjin climbed onto it, Börte behind him, holding on tightly.

~~~

Back at the camp, we admired what plunder we had won and settled down to celebrate victory. Jamuka took most of our earnings for himself while leaving the rest for Temüjin. Nekhii and I sat by the fire and discussed the battle, complaining that we had fought yet received nothing from the treasure collected.

"Soldiers!" Everyone looked up in synchrony at a man standing beside the pile of goods. He had a wide grin on his face and Temüjin was walking away in the other direction to the celebration of the leaders behind the speaker.

"Soldiers! Temüjin is good to us and shares his plunder with us!"

At first there was silence, but it was quickly followed by cheers and claps. The news went around quickly, and soon the pile had been sorted through, the best items left for Temüjin as a sign of gratitude and the rest given out amongst the soldiers. Separate piles were made for the families of the soldiers lost.

I managed to grab for myself a magnificent bow and a set of carved arrows. I tried out the bow, and found it was perfect.

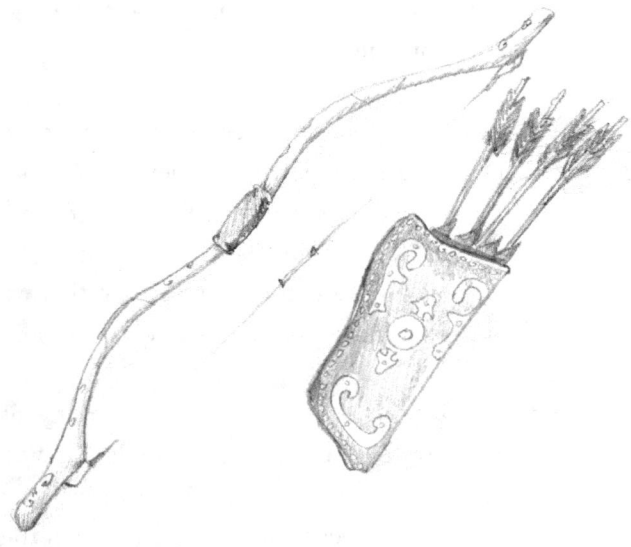

Nekhii arrived with a new hat made with white wolf's fur. It was rather nice. He sat down beside me, appearing to be genuinely happy. He wasn't fully drunk yet, but he had drank enough to loosen his tongue. His eyes contained a hint of conspiracy. I immediately knew he was up to something.

"I am joining Temüjin."

That one sentence created havoc in my head. Nekhii looked decided and his statement seemed to hide some sort of message.

"Do you want to come too?" There was the hidden message.

It was madness, switching leaders on a whim. Of course it was allowed, but no-one dared to do it. I thought of what Jamuka would do to me if he found out. Then I thought of what he would do to me regularly if I stayed.

"All right. Temüjin is good and fair, he'll treat us right. Let's do this. We'll leave with him when he goes." I nodded as I said this to my friend. We shook hands as if promising that should we go down, we would go down together. Settling to sleep, aching from the fighting, we awaited the sunrise with impatience.

In the morning, we heard shuffling, and on opening our eyes, we found Temüjin leaving earlier than expected. As we began to prepare our horses, we saw that we were not alone. Almost half of Jamuka's men were also preparing themselves. I gaped until one of the soldiers nearest me exclaimed:

"Did you think you were the only one who was tired of our Khan?" I didn't answer, simply continued to pack my things. Jumping onto my horse and following the mass of people who were trotting behind Temüjin and Börte, it looked to me as if Temüjin wasn't even surprised at the horde of people behind him. We set out into the sunrise, leaving Jamuka and the rest still asleep behind us.

My head ached and I felt suddenly dizzy. The bare greenness around me turned and turned and dissolved into brighter colours, spiraling out. I felt tugged and the reds and blues and yellows called out to me, beckoning me to them. I was sucked in and I was falling yet floating at the same time. Where will I go now?

6

A Pagan Tyranny

It is still to this day unknown how and when Christianity was introduced into Gaul, modern day France. It can only be assumed that the first missionaries came from the sea and travelled up the Rhone, reaching the city of Lugdunum, modern day Lyon. The Church of Lyon was the first church to be organised in Gaul. At the time, roman emperors were proclaimed gods, however, once Christianity began spreading, the Gauls refused to pay taxes to an emperor who claimed divinity, for there was only one god to them. The Romans were alarmed; a great part of their empire would not accept their roman deities, but more importantly, money wasn't being received. The emperor at the time, Marcus Aurelius, persecuted the Christians, first forbidding them from entering into certain public places. When they still refused to accept the Roman gods, they were thrown into the arena and tortured, while the city watched in amusement. Only one text describing such a persecution at Lyon still exists. It was written *by Eusebius, and tells the story of Blandina, a 16 year old servant girl. She was among the hundreds of other Christians scheduled to be tortured until they renounced their god and accepted the Roman ones. The young slave girl served as a martyr for her people, and less than fifty years later, there were churches seen everywhere in Roman Gaul. Blandina was supposedly the last Christian the Romans had captured to be tortured in the arena.*

I instantly jumped into his skin and I knew everything. I knew where and who I was from the memories in my newest brain. I bustled my way through the hordes of people, carefully carrying my wrapped up parcel. It was a hot summer's day, and my grey tunic was already sticking to the sweat on my body. The sky was blue and cloudless; the perfect day to take off work. I arrived at the entrance, and gave two coins to the man working there, waiting for him to bite them and make sure they were legitimate. With a nod of his head he gestured to his right, and I stepped through the entrance guarded by Roman soldiers. Once safely inside the amphitheatre, I looked back at the line of people pushing and shoving each other to enter. I was glad to be out of the hustle, and I made my way to the stone seats. I sat where a guard told me to sit, and smiled politely at the person sitting next to me. He was in his late forties, wearing a dirty, white toga. The musty scent of wine hung about him. He smiled a toothless, somewhat annoyed smile, and I knew not to start a conversation with him.

The rows of seats were being filled up rapidly, with people settling down to watch the games. The amphitheatre was fuller than usual, I saw. Guards forced families to share single spaces to provide more seats. Understandable, I thought, as today was not a usual Gladiator game. Today was to be the trial of the last two captured Christians. A young girl and a young boy. I asked myself why they were being so obtuse. They knew that if they declared they were Christians, they would be tortured. Yet they continued to pop up.

My business was blooming and I had been as busy as a man could be, baking bread day and night. This was the first game I could come to, and I was glad to have a seat, even if the slab of rock was as hot as the fires of Mars under the wide, burning sun. I unwrapped my linen parcel and peered in at the contents while waiting for the arena to fill up and the show to start.

I carefully took out the clay gourd, and took a swig of the wine I had managed to keep below lukewarm.

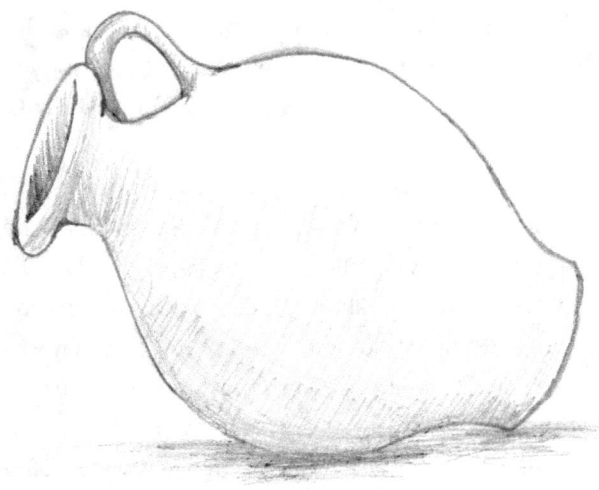

The man sitting beside me noticed, or perhaps heard the sloshing liquid, and he gave me the wide friendly smile he had somehow not managed to show before. His eyes trailed down to the gourd and he licked his dry lips. He looked back up at me and I looked steadily at him while I put the gourd down on the ground close to my feet. He scowled, but left it at that and turned his head away to gaze at the sand in the arena. I promptly ignored him as well. I pulled out a clay pot and took out one of the two pieces of bread soaked in olive oil I had. The other one would be for later. I pulled out the last of my clay pots and peeked into it, checking to make sure the half cooked meat wasn't turning in the heat. It seemed all right, so I replaced the pots in my sheet of fabric. I was still munching my bread, but I took another gulp of wine just to spite my neighbour, glancing sideways at the jealous expression he was giving me.

A horn sounded, and the entire amphitheatre grew silent. Everyone's eyes were on the lions' entrance. Out came four guards, two for each prisoner. The guards only seemed needed, however, to hold them up. The young boy, perhaps fifteen, was wearing a ragged tunic, the clothing barely covering him. He was brown with dirt and blood. The girl was even worse. My eyes strained to see the details of the tiny people so far away. Her tunic had been ripped, and her legs were showing. One sleeve had been torn, and her right breast was visible. Both prisoners were in a pitiful state.

The guards threw them in the general direction of the Emperor, and both fell to their knees from the shove. Three of the men retreated to near the closed gate, and stood with their backs to the gate. The Emperor stood up and asked a question, which

59

was relayed in a much louder voice by a spokesman. "Do you renounce your false god, and accept our deities?"

The guard pulled up the boy from the ground, and, as the slave stood there quivering, he weakly muttered an answer. The guard looked up at the Emperor and passed his hand across his thick neck in a slicing motion. The Emperor waved his hand and the boy was brought to one of the three pillars planted in the sand. He was whipped by the same guard who had relayed his answer, and, after five minutes, people watching grew impatient and started chattering. I took out a piece of meat and drank some more wine. Whipping was so boring.

The amphitheatre hushed as the guard leaned close to the boy. He must have asked the question again, but didn't receive the desired answer because he waved to the other men at the gate. One of them exited the arena and returned with two servants carrying a large stone platform covered with a wood pile. On the platform, above the wood, was placed an iron chair. It consisted of bars melded together and once the wood was lit, the flames licked the iron. Soon, the chair glowed red.

The boy was detached from the pole and brought to the center of the arena, where he was met by the servants carrying the platform. They set it down and hurried out of sight. The guard turned torturer brought the poor boy to the chair.

Blood curdling screams rang out. The boy was lifted off of the chair, asked the question again, then placed back onto the red-hot chair. After several minutes, the screams died down, and the guard shook the limp body of the boy. Two guards ran up and took the battered body, shoving it into a corner to be taken care of later.

The audience's attention then diverted to the remaining Christian. It seemed she had not moved from her spot, until the guards dragged her towards the poles and tied her up. This time, there were no whips.

The entire audience, including me, was tense with anticipation, and I was leaning in towards the show, my heart skipping beats. An opening in the arena creaked open, and four lions came out. The male emerged first, taking in everything with his beady black eyes. He was closely followed by three females. They looked good, not like the usual starved lions released in the ring. They trotted up to the poles, where they knew something would be there for them. They circled the girl, who had not uttered a sound since she was dragged in.

The male went in close to her, stayed there for a while, within an arm's length of her. Finally, he turned his back on the girl and was followed by the lionesses. They settled in a huddle in the sand, quite far away from their food. One lioness got up and went to sniff the boy who was still abandoned in a corner. Eventually, she turned him down as well and went back to the others. The four lions laid there, panting in the heat.

The previously quiet amphitheatre erupted with sound. The entire audience, including the Emperor and myself, stood up and exclaimed their anger. A great number of guards came into the arena and forced the lions out by means of whips and shouts. I was outraged. This was the first time lions had refused to eat. A little voice in my head reminded me that they had been fed hundreds of Christians in less than a month, and I almost understood why they would not want to eat any more. To rectify, the girl was whipped from all sides, tearing away whatever was left of her clothing. She began to bleed heavily, strips of red on her skin visible even from the great distance at which I was seated. Eventually the guards stopped, and one stepped up to the Christian to ask the question. She must have said no, because the man threw his arms in the air, and spat at her. He yelled instructions at his fellow guards, and within a few seconds they came back into the arena with a large net.

The spitting guard tied down the girl and wrapped her tightly in the net. The guards ran out, and for a moment, the audience was confused. What kind of torture was this?

Then, two huge, black bulls ran into the arena. They circled the area, running frantically. They spotted the net, and rammed into it. The servant was thrown high up in the air, again and again. After a while, I realised she must be dead. No screams were heard, unlike for the boy. The bulls were tossing a limp bundle. The guards must have thought the same, because they guided the bulls back out of the ring. They unwrapped the red, dripping bundle, and, to everyone's surprise, the girl stood up.

She stood up very slowly, but she did it all the same. The men stared at her for a second, and then after asking her to renounce her god once again, they sat her on the red-hot iron chair, the fire rekindled with new logs. I expected her to scream even louder than the boy, but no sound came out. I wondered if she was mute, but she couldn't be; she had talked to the guards, clearly telling them no. The man beside me had sniggered with every toss in the air the girl had suffered, but now he simply stared at her with anger and confusion.

The guards took the girl off of the chair with difficulty. Her flesh had melted to the iron, and she was stuck like honey sticks to fingers. I was disgusted by now. The heat was unbearable, my wine was boiling, the meat had turned, and now surely she had suffered enough. Had all other Christians been tortured in this way? I was afraid I knew the answer all too well. I made myself watch, unable to simply walk out of the arena. The guards had turned to brute force, punching the girl in the face and stomach. There wasn't much left of either, but she still stood, and she still refused to renounce Christianity. The guard looked up at the Emperor, who gave a nod. The man took out his knife and slowly slit the girl's throat. She crumpled to the floor, scratching at her throat, until she finally lay still in a patch of stained sand.

Dull whispers grew into chatter as everyone prepared to leave. I bundled up my parcel and held it close to my chest. I shuffled slowly out of the amphitheatre, following the line of people.

I contemplated what I had seen. I wondered if it was a good thing I had missed the previous Christian games. I hadn't enjoyed seeing the girl's torture, although I took pleasure in betting in the Gladiator games. I was finally out of the theatre and I passed several food stands.

I overheard a small child ask for a loaf of bread from a baker. The baker spat at the child and exclaimed: "I won't serve no orphan child of a Christian!" The poor child starting crying while stumbling away. Many people gave the baker a look of approval. I walked alongside the boy, and whispered down at him to follow me, I would get him bread. His water-filled eyes looked up at me. Suddenly, he smiled.

I walked in direction of my shop, with the boy following at a short distance behind me. It wasn't right to torture and persecute Christians that much, as well as starve their children, still too young to even understand religion.

I knew what would happen to my business if people knew I was serving Christians, which is why I went about it secretly. Christians had the right to taste bread made from Ceres' fields of corn. I turned a corner, and went into my shop, the boy waiting outside around a corner. He was smart.

I came back with a great loaf of olive bread, and the boy gave me a coin, hardly worth even a slice of bread. I told him to keep it, and he wandered off down the road, carrying the bread under his clothes.

The grey and brown streets around me turned and turned and they dissolved into brighter colours, spiraling out. I felt tugged and the reds and blues and yellows called out to me, beckoning me to them. I was sucked in and I was falling yet floating at the same time. Where will I go now?

7

Looking for a Judy

During the year of 1888, a fear frenzy spread throughout London, and more specifically, Whitechapel. This frenzy was caused by the almost mythical Jack the Ripper, who is claimed responsible for multiple murders and many alleged ones. Jack supposedly killed prostitutes, most of them middle-aged, and had a distinctive characteristic of gutting his victims after having slit their throats. For some of the victims, organs went missing. Whitechapel, the place where the murders happened, was the filthiest and poorest section of London, filled with the worst criminals and most unfortunate people. The police were baffled as to the sudden surge of prostitutes killed, and they were highly criticised for their perceived inactivity. Some residents of Whitechapel thought the police to be so inefficient that they started a Whitechapel Vigilance Committee, which procured private detectives and did their own patrols of the streets. Five prostitutes are considered as official victims of Jack the Ripper: Mary Ann Nichols, Annie

Chapman, Elizabeth Stride, Catherine Eddowes, and the most notorious, Mary Jane Kelly. Mary Jane Kelly was the most savage of the five, as she was killed and slowly taken apart in her apartment, compared to the usual quick guttings in the street, differing greatly from Jack's usual modus operandi. Comparatively, she was the youngest and the prettiest of the bunch. To this day, people do not know the true identity of Jack the Ripper, but plenty enjoy making careers out of finding out. However, Jack the Ripper is still known to us now not only because of the mystery of his identity, but also because of the state he put London in during that year of 1888.

I instantly jumped into her skin and I knew everything. I knew where and who I was from the memories in my newest brain.

It was dark. I let my eyes adjust to the blackness of the bedroom and looked to my right. My husband snored loudly, and I could see his dandruff clearly, regardless of the darkness. Sometimes I wondered why I still loved the great oaf. Suddenly, I heard a scream from outside my window. I froze up, not daring to move for fear of making too much noise. I heard the same scream again, but kept listening as it turned into a shrill laugh and passed under the window sill and further down the street. My husband's sleep had not been stirred. I tried relaxing my muscles, but in vain.

I was too scared, but of what I wondered? I did not live in Whitechapel, and the only person I knew who did live there would surely not be a victim. Would she? Surely she was not a prostitute? My mind pondered uselessly at the questions it was asking itself until I finally fell into a troubled sleep full of dark shadows and wandering people.

The next morning, I awoke a little later than usual, whereas my husband was still snoring loudly. I got dressed and went to the breakfast table, only to refuse the buttered scones the maid had set out on the table. I sipped my tea, but my stomach churned at the thought of anything at all. I put the tea down. Eventually, my husband joined me, still only half dressed, closely followed by my father, himself fully dressed.

I kept my eyes on my tea, although my stomach took this as an insult and protested violently to the cup in front of me. Regardless, I refused to make eye contact with my father, even while he addressed me with his usual, cold, distant manner.

"Did you sleep well, Madam?"

"Rather."

That marked the end of our daily conversation, after which we each went our own ways.

Leaving the breakfast table to work on my needlepoint, I tried to conjure up the courage to face my father, without leaving it at the proper English greetings in the morning like I always did. Somehow, the thought of my dear sister along with the memory of my dreams the night before brought me the courage I needed, and doubling back towards the kitchen, and then the study on finding him gone from the breakfast table, I knocked three times on the study door. He answered gruffly for me to enter, and stiffened his posture as I opened the door.

He got up from his chair and stood by the fireplace, ablaze to fight the bitter morning weather. After a pause during which neither of us spoke, I lifted my gaze from the floor and looked him directly in the eyes as I confronted him.

"You must stop this ridiculous antipathy towards Becky."

At the mention of the name, he turned away from the fireplace to face me so quickly that I took a step back. His eyes bore straight into mine with fearful animosity.

"I have already told you never to mention that name

whilst in my presence! And never mention it out of my presence either!"

His sudden outburst shook my courage, but it soon came flooding back when I was suddenly filled with a horrible premonition concerning my sister. I spoke out loudly, unconsciously mimicking his tone and voice:

"I will not forget my sister, whom you, sir, have condemned. She made a terrible mistake driven by lust, a common human weakness, and now surely everything she has suffered since then is enough punishment!"

"I will not hear any more of-"

"Yes, you will! Rebecca is a part of this family, and I will not have her stay in that dreadful place any longer." I took a deep breath before continuing on.

"Especially with Jack the Ripper." At this last remark, my father lifted up his eyes, and I could see they were full of sadness. He said weakly, before his image of a strong, respectable gentleman took over:

"Surely she would not become a victim. She is not a prostitute. She is not a prostitute, is she? Is she?!"

"Prostitute or not, what if she sees the killer and is silenced by him?! I do not need anymore of your excuses and prejudices! I am going to fetch her with or without your permission. Disinherit me too for all I care!" I stormed out of the house, my father too dumbstruck to try to stop me, and hailed a cab.

"Where's to, ma'am?"

"Whitechapel."

"The Chapel? Eh, that might not be a good idea considerin' yur class and the times an' all, ma'am." I glared at the driver, still fuming from my altercation with my father, reminded him of his position, and the coachman said no more.

~~~

We eventually arrived, as I could tell by the stench and the shady characters lurking against the walls. The coachman drove me as far as a popular pub, and once I had paid him, he took off into a dark alley with a scantily clad woman, who greedily took the coins I had just passed on to the driver.

People had started to gather around me; men with knives held to their chins, using them to eat rotten apples; women staying in groups and whispering to each other and giggling. My rage had since then disappeared, and I hurried into the pub, hoping to be safer in there than in the street.

Once I entered, everyone became quiet except for some drunken man still singing a sailor's song. Eventually, everyone resumed their conversations and I was mostly ignored, apart from the occasional nervous glances made in my direction. I walked to the bartender and tried to casually ask about my sister.

"Excuse me, sir? Might I inquire you about a certain individual who lives around here? Going by the name of Rebecca?"

"Ain't know anyone by that name."

"Please, you must help me, she is slightly shorter than me, has auburn hair?"

"Lookie 'ere ma'am, I ain't know of no Rebecca, b'sides, what the bloody 'ell is *auburn* 'air? Keep yur fancy words for yur fancy friends, 'ere ain't nothing but the common folk who get butchered while yur sippin' on yur bloody tea! Now, you gonna order a drink'r'not?"

Irked by the bartender's aggressiveness, I decided to order a gin, just to keep him from striking out again. However, once it had been served, I found myself actually drinking it. Suddenly emboldened by the alcohol, I pressed the bartender further. I had also begun to talk louder.

"Now, *you* look *here*! I need to find Becky! She lives in Whitechapel, she is slightly shorter than me and she has *brownish-reddish* hair. She is twenty years old now! I need to find her!"

At this point, the bartender ignored me as he did

his other drunk customers, but before I could order another gin out of frustration, a rather ugly and scrawny man came up to me. He had a limp eye which I couldn't help but stare at.

"I 'ear you're lookin' for a Judy."

"No, I'm looking for a Rebecca."

"Ye, ye, a Judy what like. Beck's one of me Judies." His thick cockney accent and his limp eye hindered my understanding.

"I... I don't comprehend what you're saying. Who is Judy, and have you seen the woman I'm looking for?" The man rolled the one good eye he had and tried to explain to me what he was proposing, all the while most probably trying to figure out what 'comprehend' meant.

"Youse lookin' for a Judy, a whore, a... what youse posh people call 'em? A prosty? Naw, tha' ain't it."

"Do you mean a prostitute?"

"Ye, ye! That's it!"

"But what does a prostitute have to do with Rebecca?" The man gave me a confounded look and said:

"Well, Beck is a Judy. I knows her, I do." Before continuing on, he adopted a sly smile.

"I'm wha' you migh' call her protector o' sorts. 'Mongst other things. Never be too careful, especial with wha' 's been goin' on 'round 'ere."

I must have fainted, because the next thing I knew, I was lying on the floor with people around me, some disgusted, some laughing, and I could taste brandy on my lips. My face hurt, most likely from a slap the ugly man had given me.

"Youse alrigh'?" I brushed his hand away from my face, trying not to show the revulsion I felt at his touch.

"Yes, yes, I'm quite alright. I need you to take me to Becky."

"Sure, sure. But lets me tell ya, youse the strangest client I've 'ad for her. She don' usually 'ake women."

I decided to ignore his comment, and let him believe I was a client – I shuddered at the very thought – for the moment, and a concern began to overwhelm me as we left the pub and walked in the shadiest and worst looking alleyway of them all. Would this man let me take Becky away? Surely she was so pretty as to be the highest income he gained? But I was struck by another thought, one I had completely forgotten about, and one that I dreaded. Who was this man I was following into an alleyway? How was I to trust a single thing he said?

I hardly had time enough to ponder the question, when I was shaken from my thoughts by sudden shouting. Two men, walking towards us, were handing out leaflets and shouting at the tops of their voices.

"Fourth victim of the Whitechapel Killer! Fourth murder! Join the Whitechapel Vigilance committee! Lock yer doors! Stay off the street!"

They stopped a minute and shook hands with my companion.

"'Ow you doin' there Smith?"

"No' too bad there, lads."

"Say, who's the lass? Seems 'igh class for a chap like you." They gave a lecherous glance which I did not appreciate at all, but they intimidated me in such a way that I did not reply. I dropped my eyes to the ground.

"Ah, a client for one of the gurls." The committee members nodded knowingly, and said goodbye.

"Well, take care of yurself. And say 'ello to the girls for us. Make sure youse lock yer doors, need to protect you and yours." One of the men gave a wink and they continued on, resuming their shouting.

We also continued on our way, despite my fears, and we arrived at the end of the alleyway before I had time to realise it. My companion knocked five times on a door half hidden in the shadows. He gruffly muttered a few words to the door, most likely a passcode, and the door swung open.

I almost fainted again, but I just barely escaped the hands of my unconscious.

Inside was a dimly lit room, about the size of half of my drawing room; that is, very small, and it was littered with women of all types, lounging around. Most were wearing close to nothing. They did not seem surprised to see me. The few men that were there were so doped on opium that they could only barely open their eyelids. My lungs protested at the smoke-filled air, and I began to feel lightheaded from the second-hand fumes.

I saw Becky, in a corner, napping, an opium pipe beside her. The man who had brought me here was talking to me, but I did not listen. I felt disgust at first, but relief replaced disgust, hope replaced relief, and horror hope. She was thinner than I remembered, and was losing her hair. Her lovely hair. I let out a croak and stumbled towards her. I shook her to wake her up, and called out her name. She reeked of liquor, and her nose and cheeks were red with it. Her droopy eyelids lifted high enough to see me, and I was once again filled with relief as she recognised me.

"Sissy?"

"Yes, it's me, dear."

"What are you doin' 'ere?"

"I'm here to save you honey, I'm here to save you." She had slightly lost her accent, but she was still my Becky. I carried as much of her weight as I could, but was forced to halt when the ugly man blocked my path. He was shouting something. I didn't care what, I didn't even care about his limp eye, or the spit he was sending flying as he screamed. The others in the room were now all staring at what was happening, but I didn't much care about that either. I simply reached into my pocket and pulled out the money bag I always carried with me.

The man continued talking but less aggressively as he saw the bag and heard the tinkle of coins. I threw a random handful at his feet, at which point he had completely stopped talking and began scooping the almost five pounds[1] I had thrown at him.

Becky had started drifting back to sleep, so I stirred her and we continued on. After returning to the pub, I managed to hail a coach and we began the journey home. I couldn't help stroking Becky's hair on the ride back.

Once we reached home, my father was in the hallway. He took a look at the both of us, gave a curt nod, and let us through, without saying a word. I set my poor, dear, little sister into her bed, which had still been entertained, even after her elopement, and I sung her a lullaby.

"You're safe here, Becky, I'll protect you. Hush now, sleep." And so she did.

~~~

The very next morning, the papers were selling like hot buns. The latest and worst to date of Jack the Ripper's victims had been found, a certain Mary Jane Kelly. She had been killed and butchered in

---

1 The cost of living in Victorian times was a lot lower than it is today, and one pound then would make very, very roughly 30 modern pounds, but consider that less than a pound would be spent a week on liquor by a moderate drinker, i.e., a bottle a day.

her apartment, 13 Miller's Court, 26 Dorset Street, Whitechapel, only a street away from where I had found Becky.

I laid in bed next to my dear sister, still asleep, hugging her, and the room around me turned and turned and it dissolved into brighter colours, spiraling out. I felt tugged and the reds and blues and yellows called out to me, beckoning me to them. I was sucked in and I was falling yet floating at the same time. Where will I go now?

8

Coming to a Decision

The French Revolution is arguably one of the most important moments of French history. It all started quite slowly and progressively. When Louis XVI inherited the throne along with his Austrian wife, Marie Antoinette, France was already destitute. It had just finished fighting in a war, and the people were hungry. However, instead of immediately fixing the problem, the rulers of the nation raised the taxes on the poor. Finance ministers came and went for a long while, and every time one would mention that the poor had no more money and that instead taxes should be raised for the higher classes, they would be fired. In addition to the taxes, Marie Antoinette, who was still a very frivolous princess in her mind, spent like crazy and enjoyed the finer things in life. Although not very evil, she became the scourge of the entire population, and she was the very symbol of anti-freedom and anti-rights. It's no surprise that the financial situation aggravated, and the people of France had just had enough. Now *faced with dramatic conditions, the King decided to reinstate the Estates-General, a sort of grouping of each class (clergy, noble, commoners) which was charged with the task of finding a solution to the depression. Votes would be decided by one vote per group instead of one vote per head. It was then that the lower class truly realised how powerless they were, for they knew full well the clergy and nobles would always stay together. The Third Estate (the commoners) wanted to have a meeting to discuss this powerlessness, but when denied such a meeting without the presence of the other estates, the group rushed to a tennis court and held its meeting there, on the 20th of June, 1789, while making an oath to always stay together and protect the interests of France and her people. The members of the Third Estate renamed themselves the National Assembly, and it was from there on that the rioting and plotting for power and constant hunger of the people brought the Reign of Terror, famous for guillotine executions of anyone even suspected of being against the current government, which shifted constantly, or anyone who was in the way of a political plot. In the middle of this we find Jacques-Louis David, a painter and friend of Maximillien Robespierre, a main revolutionary leader held* responsible for the guillotine executions. David was the only painter at the time to decide to capture the Revolution as it happened, giving us the paintings we commonly use when discussing the Revolution. However, his drawings also brought along problems for everyone. When he became involved with politics and voted for the death of the King, his Royalist wife divorced him, he was marked as an enemy by the Royalists, and at the end of Robespierre's rule, he was imprisoned. His paintings in general contained messages alluding to freedom, the constitution and anti-monarchy; the people of France adopted them as national symbols of the Revolution. Robespierre was guillotined himself in 1794 after he was overthrown, at which point Napoleon took the chance of swooping in with a coup d'état, and proclaimed himself Emperor of France. Napoleon began releasing people from prison, and took a liking to

David and vice-versa, and it is again from David that
we have our paintings of iconic Napoleon moments.
When Napoleon fell from power, David's life was
again threatened. As Louis XVIII, Louis XVI's
brother, came back to power, he and other Royalists
intended to take revenge on all their enemies.

I instantly jumped into her skin and I knew everything. I knew where and who I was from the memories in my newest brain. My hand continued weaving the needle in and out of the fabric, the smooth movement calming me. I tried to weave quietly, straining my ears to listen to the conversation in the next room.

Looking about me, I put my work aside and got up from my chair. The floor squeaked under my feet, something it seemed only to do when I was trying to be quiet. I approached the door slowly, moving ear first, trying to hear better without getting too close. Eventually, I was forced to place my ear on the lavish carved wooden door, and was only then able to hear what was going on inside.

"I think it's too risky."

"It's your only choice. Think about it."

Suddenly, I heard oncoming footsteps and quickly ran back to my seat, only not quickly enough. I was halfway to the chair when the door handle turned, so I whipped around and pretended I was about to walk up to the door. The effect was slightly hindered by my fast breathing, and I was sure the guest could hear my heart beating. The guest saw me breathless, a few feet away from the door, and immediately assumed a scowl. He looked over his shoulder to my husband, and shouted out.

"And keep your wife in line!"

The guest scoffed, looked back at me, scowled again, and walked quickly past me towards the door.

Hearing the entrance slam, I proceeded into Jacques-Louis' studio. He was sitting at his stool, made very small in contrast with the four by five meter canvas. His hand gently applied red to a cape on a strong muscular Spartan.

"He's right you know. You shouldn't eavesdrop." He looked up from his painting.

"I don't understand why I shouldn't be a part of the discussion. It's my future too."

"You aren't allowed for the same reason that the children aren't." He looked back to his painting. There was a silence, until I spoke up.

"Well?"

"Well what?"

"What did he say?"

"You were eavesdropping, you should know."

"I barely heard the last few words." Louis, as I called him, set down his brush and turned to face me on his stool. I stayed where I was, in the entrance.

"He thinks I should beg. Not exactly the words he used, but close enough. He believes that since the signing for Louis XVI's execution was twenty years ago, it'll be long enough ago and I'm talented enough to be pardoned." I bit my lip. Sure, he was talented enough, he was proclaimed as the number one painter in France, but...

"What about Napoleon?"

"He believes that will also be forgiven."

"How could Louis XVIII forget, let alone forgive you? Napoleon humiliated him and overthrew him. And to top it all off, the *English* had to help him. He will not take to this lightly."

"But I wasn't a part of the politics that time... I was just the appointed painter."

"Do you think the Royalists will tell the difference? They'll remember you for the Reign of Terror and as a person who voted for the death of the King, and as a member of Robespierre's dictatorship. They'll remember your paintings."

Louis put on a pained expression and muttered.

"But I do not wish to leave France. If I had to, I would like to go to my dear Italy, but you know already that we were denied access. And what is with the change of opinion? I thought you did not want to leave either."

I felt tears building, but made no effort to hold them back. I knew now that staying was not an option. If I had to give up my beloved France for him to stay alive, then I would. In a despicable way, I hoped my tears would convince Louis to flee. He saw them, and his face scrunched up.

"Marguerite, do not cry. I beg of you." I wiped my eyes, which made room for additional tears to flood up. We both stared at each other for a while, until we were interrupted by a servant. She kept her head so low that I only saw her bonnet in place of her face, and she muttered about the supper being ready. I curtsied to Louis and walked out, heading for my room. Before I could reach it, Louis was running behind me, and embraced me into his arms.

"We need to talk, Marguerite."

He led me to the drawing room and sat on the settee. Sitting down beside him, I laid my head on his shoulder, and his arm went around me. I started to speak.

"I do not want you to stay here. I do not want you to become influenced by politics again. I do not want to lose you, not again."

"I can only imagine how it was for you. Perhaps you felt as tortured as I did in prison; deprived of my paints and brushes, with nothing to do."

"I did not like who you had become. You became violent, you changed. I saw no other way to protect my heart and the children."

"It's alright, I understand now, and all is well. We are re-married now." He smiled, while a thought crossed my mind and I scowled. I inched away from him.

"How could you remarry after divorcing me?" Louis gulped and tried to find an answer. He stuttered and finally said 'I love you' in a sweet voice, looking deep into my eyes. I had already forgiven him, no one could stay mad at him for long, but I decided to have a bit of fun. Scowling even harder, he searched harder for a satisfying response. Eventually, he came up with a solution:

"I shall paint your portrait. It'll be soft, and kind, and light, just like you." I smiled, and kissed him, laughing at his relieved look. He joined me in laughter and we momentarily forgot our troubles. However, we were interrupted by the maid, who came once again to tell us that supper was ready. We got up to follow her, sat in our seats at the table, and ate a lukewarm soup.

I thought of the situation, of my grown and married children, and of Louis's previous wife. I felt sorry for her, in a way. I owed her, too. She had worked so hard to get Louis out of prison. If it wasn't for her, Louis would surely have been guillotined, and we wouldn't have been able to eat supper together again as we were now doing. I wondered what had become of her.

Soon, the table was cleared and Louis and I, each at one end of the table, looked at each other in silence. We both knew that a decision had to be made. I was starting to feel uneasy at the quiet, so I asked him the first questions to come into my mind.

"What were you thinking? Why would you get caught up with the Jacobin club, and all the radicals that were in it? Of all people why did you look up to Robespierre?"

I paused, hesitating to ask the last question.

"Why did you choose political power over me?"

Louis stayed silent. He got up and settled on a chair beside me. After a moment of looking at the floor, he began to speak.

"When the Estates-General was re-instated and the Third Estate broke off, I... I was attracted to the idea of freedom, and equality. I enjoyed seeing it in my paintings, but the idea of having it in real life was tantalising. I began to sketch the oath the National Assembly made in that tennis court, you know, when the King denied them access to the meeting room. But before I could finish it, riots broke out, and the King fired the Finance Minister Necker, and the Assembly retaliated, and... and then the Bastille was taken over. I was surprised at the violence, but I was also amazed by it. We were standing up to our oppressors, Marguerite, surely you can understand the appeal in that." I kept silent and he continued on.

"Everything went so quickly. I just flowed along with it. The peasants against the army, the army with the peasants, the panic, the fear. Then the Constitution came along. It was amazing. We had taken power for ourselves, at the expense of the nobles."

I did not like how Louis still marvelled at the Revolution. I was about to interject something when he started up again.

"But then the King and his family ran away. The Constitution couldn't let that be. After the royal family was placed in isolation, it was decided that we should remove all traces of a monarchy. I agreed. I... I voted for his death." He looked up from the floor and stared right into my eyes, startling me.

"I do not regret it, Marguerite. However much you find it wrong, I do not regret it. I know France will become better because of it." He looked back at the floor.

"It was then that my paintings begun to have stronger messages in them. I painted Hercules with an aim to bring hope, and managed to become famous. I am somewhat proud of that. I tried my luck at politics, but..."

"But I divorced you."

"Well, yes."

There was an awkward silence until Louis continued. "When Robespierre and I met, his loyalty to the Revolution struck me. It was incomparable. He truly did want the best for France. He wanted a pure, rich and good France. The same as Marat, may they both rest in peace. I see now that the ultimate Utopia is not obtainable, but you cannot reproach me for admiring those who tried."

"You neglect to mention that the 'pure' France Robespierre wanted is stained with blood, at his hand, and at Napoleon's. I do not consider that good and pure."

"Robespierre was too blinded by the prize of the race to see that he was cheating to win."

"Cheating? Is that what you call sentencing men, women and children to death on mere suspicions? For everyone knows that most of the arrests were made on flimsy or non-existent evidence." There was yet another uneasy silence.

"May I continue?"

I nodded.

"My reaction to Napoleon was very much like my reaction to Robesp –, well, I admired Napoleon too. He held the ideals that were the cause of the revolution in the first place. When he gave himself power, although I was surprised, I was happy that he chose to appoint me as his official painter. Working for him was rather hard, though. He always wanted the most ludicrous changes to be made! But I'm afraid that like Robespierre, and Caesar, and Alexander the Great, all kingdoms must come to an end. However, now, with the restoration of the Monarchy, I fear not just for my safety. Does this restoration mean that it was all for naught? The riots, the death, the Revolution?"

I placed my hand on Louis' shoulder and waited for him to say it. We both knew what decision had to be made. It was irrefutable. Louis spoke softly.

"I guess there is no choice. We must not risk it. We shall leave."

~~~

A fortnight later, we were packing our belongings. I was happy; I was sad to leave France, but I was glad for the new start. I turned to Louis.

"Can you read me the letter again?"

"Again?!"

"Please."

"I already put it away."

"Then remind me of the contents."

"Fine. Dear Monsieur David, we are extremely glad and honored that you would choose our humble country to live in. You are welcome to live with us, and we will offer you employment and accommodation. Something along those lines."

The carriage was announced, and putting on my coat with Louis' help, we stepped into the comfortable wagon. The door closed and we rode off. I looked through the window and said my final goodbyes to my beautiful home. Louis held my hand and whispered in my ear.

"To Belgium we go."

The carriage around me turned and turned and it dissolved into brighter colours, spiraling out. I felt tugged and the reds and blues and yellows called out to me, beckoning me to them. I was falling yet floating at the same time. Where will I go now?

9

The Marriage

The Tudor family is most known for Henry VIII and his six wives. His two headstrong daughters, Mary and Elizabeth, are equally familiar in the history books. In all, five Tudors ruled England and its kingdoms, the first one being Henry VII, who fought for the throne in battle. This War of the Roses was a sort of civil feud during which two branches of the Royal family, the York's and the Lancaster's, fought for the right to the throne. The war was named thus after the symbolic rose emblems for each family, red for Lancaster, white for York. Surprisingly, Henry Tudor, distant descendant of Edward III and an obscure member of the Lancaster's, won the battle for the throne, effectively ending the war, and uniting the two families by marrying Elizabeth of York. Henry and Elizabeth had four children who survived infancy: Arthur, Margaret, Henry and Mary, in order of birth. Henry VII immediately wanted to make strong allies to fortify his claim to the throne, and so, a marriage agreement between Catherine of

Aragon, then three, and Arthur Tudor, then two, was made with Ferdinand II of Aragon and Isabella I of Castille, Catherine's parents. Catherine left Spain to be with her new husband in 1501, and they married in the same year, Arthur at fifteen, Catherine at sixteen. However, as they settled into their new home and titles of Prince and Princess of Wales, both fell seriously ill. Arthur did not survive the illness. The Spaniards, desperate to keep the alliance, and the English desperate to keep the dowry which had only been half payed, started negotiations for another marriage: Catherine and Arthur's younger brother, Henry, new heir to the throne. After much back and forth between Ferdinand II and Henry VII, the marriage terms were still not agreed to. However, the situation changed when Henry VII died of tuberculosis in 1509. Now new King of England and free of his father, young Henry proposed to Catherine, who accepted. They were married in the same year of Henry VII's death, and had a happy relationship which lasted for almost fifteen years, regardless of Henry's mistresses. However, one mistress in particular, Anne Boleyn, decided to take the relationship further, causing havoc between Henry and Catherine, whom had undergone many years and troubles before being married.

I instantly jumped into her skin and I knew everything. I knew where and who I was from the memories in my newest brain. I felt a pinch in my side, and I gave a jolt. I looked down and saw the rugged seamstress weave a needle in my dress. She sniffed loudly and wiped her nose with her hand. She then proceeded to clean her hand on her apron.

I turned away from her and looked at my reflection. The dress hung heavily around my shoulders. I tried to relieve some of the weight, but the movement vexed my seamstress, who hurled at me. I had not yet gained knowledge of English, but nonetheless I understood, and remained still, ignoring my discomfort.

Eventually, the wedding dress was done, and it was ten fold heavier than it had been. I stepped down from the stool, and walked around. I felt my whole body being pulled down by the weight, but forced my back to stay straight. I was used to such trivial things. I was to be a Queen, after all, and beauty and power came with a price.

The seamstress left without a word, although I was hardly left to my own, for His Majesty Henry VII came in after her. I bowed low, ignoring the stiff dress preventing me from doing so, and kept my head down. His Majesty walked around me, rubbed his chin, talked to his advisors and left.

Finally left in peace, I put my hand to my forehead. I felt cold.

Could I really do it? Could I get married? It was not as if I did not know my... husband. We had already exchanged letters over the years, but nothing personal enough to account for our soon to be intimacy. I reminded myself I had no choice, and my betrothed, Prince Arthur, did not seem in any way to be spiteful or contemptible. He was a God-fearing Christian, and a good person. I knelt on the ground despite my protesting gown, and prayed to God our Lord. I prayed for mankind and to be a good ruler, although I knew that Queens seldom made decisions nor were involved in the politics of the state. I prayed to continue to be a girl of – I stopped myself. I was no longer a girl: I had started my bleeding many years ago; I was getting married; I was sixteen. I started the prayer anew and prayed to continue to be a *woman* of virtue and Godliness. But most importantly, I prayed to be happy with Arthur, who would hopefully love me as much as I was sure I would come to love him.

As I was finishing my prayer with blessings for my family in my dear Spain, I heard a knock at my door. I crossed myself, wondering who would bother to knock. I was not yet a ruler, nor a Tudor, and had so far been treated like an object to be traded and inspected. My heart skipped a beat as I wondered if it could be Prince Arthur, but I calmed myself with the thought that even if it were him, he would be with his mentor, or at least a chaperone. I made for the door, but found movement difficult and my knees were still buckled from the weight of the dress, so I called out in the only word of English I could grasp: "Y-yes?"

The doorknob turned, and to my surprise, I saw a little boy, no taller than half my height, looking up at me earnestly. His hair was ruffled, his clothes disheveled, and he had a tiny scrape along his cheek. I caught a whiff of the musty English forests I had yet to become accustomed to. His eyes opened wide as he saw me, and he gave what sounded like a gasp of delight. He closed the door behind him and shuffled his feet shyly. I smiled at him. Surely I would not be so bad here in England with such a gentle boy to care for?

"¿Qué pasa, Príncipe Enrique?" He looked up and started talking in English. He talked even faster than usual, and was continuing to shuffle his feet. I walked towards him and knelt down in front of him. I put my hand on his sturdy, yet small shoulder.

"No comprendo." I waved my head, and he seemed to understand. He looked from side to side, searching for something in his mind. Eventually he said:

"Belle. T-très belle." He pointed at me. I shuffled

back a bit and felt my cheeks blush. His cheeks also reddened. I continued in French, hoping he would understand.

"Où est ton tuteur ?" His tutor most probably had not allowed Prince Henry to see me un-chaperoned. It was against tradition, and rather improper, but I found myself liking the company. Prince Henry stumbled a bit, but he managed to give an answer.

"Je me suis enfuis." So he ran away? But why go to all that trouble? I gave him a quizzical look.

He looked into my eyes before running around me, tripping over the trail of my dress. I went to pick him up, but he got up himself, passing his hand through his hair, ruffling it even further. He avoided eye contact and continued to run to the other side of the room. He grabbed a piece of paper and wrote on it using the quill and ink that was beside it. While I heard the scritch scratch of the quill on parchment, I attempted to stand back up, but I had knelt for so long, that my knees were solid as stone, and did not respond well to my commands. I staggered up and let myself fall into a nearby chair, not caring much about organising the dress. I closed my eyes and waited. Suddenly, the scritch scratch stopped, and I opened my eyes. Prince Henry was in front of me, paper in hand. He said a few words

I couldn't understand and handed me the note.
I read it quickly, the latin being simple enough to
understand. Written in an elegant hand, it read a
message along the lines of:

Dear Catherine,

I am sorry to have to say this in a letter. I will
learn Spanish, and then we will be able to
converse in person. I am telling you not to be sad.
If Prince Arthur mistreats you, remember that
I will watch over you. I know you will make
a wonderful Queen. I will stand by you. I am
ten, but that does not matter to me. I am strong,
I am stronger than my meek brother. Be Happy.

Your watchful companion forever,
Henry

I finished reading the note and felt a tear trickle
down my face. Dear little Henry looked worriedly
at me. I smiled at him and beckoned him into my
arms. He walked slowly, awkwardly, to get to where
I was on my chair. Once within reach, I grabbed
him, to his great surprise, and settled him on my lap.
I gave him a great big hug, to which he also put his

arms around me. Suddenly, my seamstress came in the room, and she gave a shriek at what she saw. She ran out, hands clasped around her face. I vaguely wondered if she was alarmed at my un-ladylike behaviour with a young prince, or at how creased the dress had become. Still sitting on my lap, Henry broke away from my arms, and looking at each other, we both laughed. He got up, and standing in front of me, helped me get up and fix my dress. Once looking more suitable, I curtseyed as low as I could, and getting up, looked straight down in Prince Henry's eyes and said the only other phrase I had grasped in English.

"Thank you, Príncipe Enrique." He blushed and looked at the floor. Not as surprising as the first time, the seamstress came in, this time followed by a stern looking man, dressed entirely in black. He said a few words to the seamstress who reclined in the shadows of the room, then said some more to Henry, who looked defiant. The man grabbed Henry's arm and led him out, but not before Henry could sneak a smile at me. The grave man nodded curtly at me before leaving with my young friend. The seamstress came out from the shadows, and muttering to herself, she began to work on my dress once again.

This time, I did not contemplate the crushing weight of the gown, nor the overwhelming smell of the seamstress. I kept my back straight, my chin up, and stood proud. Before I knew it, the woman had gone, and I was left alone. I took out my letter and read it again. I pressed it to my heart, and then, thinking of my future and Prince Henry's, I placed it in the kindling fire. The flames raged once again as they consumed the new fuel. I felt my spirit being uplifted, and I waited patiently in the room, the dress fanned out neatly about me.

Eventually, there was a knock, but before I could wonder if Prince Henry had run away again, a stranger came in without waiting for an answer. Behind the stranger was my ambassador, and behind the ambassador was Henry, grinning sheepishly. Behind Henry was the grim faced man who clearly disliked Henry's attitude and demeanor. My ambassador informed me the ceremony was beginning, and I was led by the group into the hallways, turning left or right on occasion. I walked straight, my handmaids carrying my trail behind me. I felt, and looked like a Queen.

I stopped in front of a closed door, and Henry coming by my side, took my arm. He was dressed eloquently, and looking behind him at his tutor, he glanced up at me with an earnest smile. The doors opened and we were faced with a great hall, full of people. The priest waited at the altar, bible in hand, and off to the side was Prince Arthur, along with His Majesty Henry VII.

Suddenly, I was overwhelmed with the faces of everyone looking at me. In an instant, I saw my entire life play out. I was scared of all the plots, the conspiracies, the games, the lies, the sadness, the children, everything I would be subjected to. I froze in place. Would I be strong enough to withstand all the pain and heartache after all? My education and preparation would surely be useless.

I snapped out of my stupor when I felt a slight pressure on my arm. I looked at Prince Henry, who looked back up.

I took a deep breath and walked down the aisle, arm in arm with Prince Henry, and without hesitation I walked tall towards my fate. No matter the hardships, I would have a faithful companion to watch over me. I smiled inwardly. Everything would be perfectly fine. For a while anyway.

The altar in front of me turned and turned and it dissolved into brighter colours, spiraling out. I felt tugged and the reds and blues and yellows called out to me, beckoning me to them. I was falling yet floating at the same time. Where will I go now?

10

A Request

King Philip IV of France, known as Philip the Fair, was crowned in 1286. During his reign, the French treasury began to run dangerously low, and the kingdom was in heavy debt. One of these debts was to the Knights Templar, which had been acting as a bank for almost two hundred years while crusades were lacking. Philip IV decided to eradicate the Templars in an effort to bury his debt, and seize the Templar treasury. Hundreds of Templars were arrested simultaneously, and most were tortured into pleading guilty to heresy, to give credence to the arrests. It was noted, however, that when Master of the Templars Jacques de Molay was publicly burned at the stake as an example, de Molay cursed Philip IV and his generations to come. The curse seemed to have come to life as the direct bloodline ran out, leaving the throne to another royal branch, in less than twenty years. Of Philip IV and his four children, Louis, Philip, Charles and Isabella, all met misfortune. Philip IV died a year after the execution of Molay, and *the throne passed through his three sons faster than wildfire. Isabella, on her side, as Queen of England by alliance, also had a rough marriage, rule and life. One particular misfortune that occured early on in the 'curse', is the Affair of the Nesle Tower. Philip (jr.) and Charles had married sisters Jeanne and Blanche de Bourgogne, respectively. Louis had married the girls' cousin, Margaret de Bourgogne. Perhaps jealous of the easygoing life of her sisters-in-law, Isabella found out and revealed Blanche and Margaret's infidelities to her father, Philip IV, in 1314. Philip IV, outraged, had both girls tried and imprisoned for life. Jeanne was also imprisoned, but put in a nicer prison, her only crime being complicity; she knew of her sister and cousin's affairs with two sibling knights, Gautier and Philippe d'Aunay (both of whom were castrated, drawn and quartered, broken on a wheel, and finally hung). The affair was named after the couples' usual rendez-vous spot: the Nesle Tower, an old watch tower. When Philip IV died and Louis X took over the throne in 1314, he immediately wanted a divorce from Margaret. The difficult-to-obtain piece of papal paper turned out to be unnecessary when Margaret died of a mysterious 'illness' while in prison. Louis remarried very soon after to secure the throne with an heir, while Philip (jr.), next in line for the throne, begged his elder brother to free Jeanne, who had only been guilty of knowing a secret. However, it was not an easy thing to get her out of her predicament. Louis still loathed Margaret, and brought into question the validity of their only daughter and subsequently of all her and her relatives actions. But Philip, known under his king title as Philip V the Tall, had very good reasons for wanting his wife back.*

I instantly jumped into his skin and I knew everything. I knew where and who I was from the memories in my newest brain. I continued fiddling with my wedding band, twisting it repeatedly around my finger. I resisted the urge to shift around in my chair, instead staring resolutely ahead. The others around me continued on in their useless bickering. I allowed myself a quick distracting glance around the vast room, following the pillar arches with my eyes. I heard silence around me in place of the usual chatter, and glanced down to observe. My brother, my King, Louis X, had his hands clenched tightly in front of him. The others seated around the table were looking at their own interlocked hands. Before I could commit the mistake of asking what had happened, thus revealing I was not paying attention, the king spoke up.

"I don't want to hear it! I will not have talk of those – *of that* – traitor. I refuse to discuss it. That is an order!"

I knew in an instant he was referring to our wives, and I glanced to the side to see Charles, the youngest of us. He had actually loved his woman, poor man. It was clearly visible that he had been upset, hurt, cried even, when he had found out Blanche de Bourgogne's infidelities. Fool.

I took a deep breath and spoke up, addressing a king.

"Your Majesty, we must resolve the matter, whether you like it or not."

The table shook as Louis banged his fists down. His

already less-than-handsome face scrunched into an even uglier expression of anger, an expression he seemed to enjoy wearing often.

"What is there to discuss?! They are in prison, and *she* is rightly dead."

"I would like Your Majesty to reconsider Jeanne de Bourgogne's imprisonment. I strongly believe that she has served her time for not revealing her sister."

Charles beside me whimpered, and everyone in the room had at once the same mixed look of pity and embarrassment in their eyes. I added:

"It was also our father's decree that they should continue to be locked away until forgiven by their respective husbands..."

I trailed my sentence, and swallowed loudly; had I actually forgiven Jeanne? My brother seemed not to notice my stutter.

"You've forgiven her now, have you?!" He spat out, echoing my thoughts.

"Leave us! All of you!"

I watched as all the counsellors and ministers got up and left the chamber, without a word of protest.

Once the door was closed behind the last person, my brother and I looked at each other. Finally, I spoke up.

"Louis, as your counsellor, I advise you to pardon Jeanne de Bourgogne."

Seeing his smirk, I rephrased.

"As your *brother*, I beg of you. Her crimes were not as traitorous."

"Ha, do you not hear your own words? As traitorous?! A traitor is still a traitor, no matter the degree of the crime! Why do you insist on that bloody woman anyway?! Why is her release so important?!"

I was about to respond when suddenly the thought struck me again. Why *was* her release important? My well reasoned answer somehow seemed lacking, all of a sudden. I just knew I had to have her back. Regardless of my doubt, I gave a conventional answer.

"I would hate to see the Franche-Comté region forever in the Bourgogne family. As I'm sure Your Highness would too, considering the financial situation."

"Why would you do such a stupid thing as to give Franche-Comté to your wife?"

"It seemed an appropriate idea at the time."

"Idiot."

We simply stared at each other, both gaging the other, until finally, Louis started to speak again. He seemed to have calmed down.

"I'll think about it. Now leave me alone. And send for my wife."

I got up and nodded curtly, turning my back to him. Without stopping, I called back over my shoulder.

"Thank you."

I had reached the door, but paused before leaving, hearing the King call out after me.

"Is that gratitude from a counsellor, or a brother?"

I smiled a little, although he did not see it, and without looking back at him, I answered:

"Both, Your Highness."

Passing the footman at the door, I asked him to send for Her Majesty Clementia of Hungary.

~~~

My room, with its tapestries, looked even more grim than usual. I locked the door, and once safe from prying eyes, I flopped on the bed, and lay on my back, legs dangling towards the floor.

My mind travelled in itself, and it brought back to light a forgotten question. Why did I want Jeanne back? For her property, surely. For her property? Yes, for her property...

Her face conjured up in my mind, and my eyes traced her delicate jawbone, and back around to the tip of her nose.

I suddenly sat up. I looked around to make sure no

one could see me. I ruffled my hand through my hair, questioning my own sanity. I needed air.

Passing through the corridors, I avoided anyone I passed, simply ignoring them if they struck up a conversation.

When I reached the gates to the garden, I paused just before the threshold. It was raining. Looking around and finding nobody, I stepped out.

The pounding of the heavy raindrops on my head seemed to do me good, and I just stood there, enjoying the monotone patter. My thoughts became blank. I forgot my troubles, my deceased father, my quick-tempered brother, the curse of the Templars, my other, weak brother, and I even forgot pressing matters of the state, such as the empty treasury, the hungry people... But I couldn't forget Jeanne. She somehow still managed to break through the wall of consciousness and manifest herself in my thoughts. I cursed the bloody woman. I realised I almost didn't want her released, if it meant continuing to doubt.

I was suddenly shaken by a shiver, and with surprise I felt my teeth chattering. A voice behind me tentatively spoke.

"Um, Your Royal Highness? Do you require anything?" A low-ranking nobleman, or rather noble*boy*, spoke with concern, although he had his head bent low.

"No."

"I was told His Majesty should like an audience with you." I nodded at the young man and went down the corridors, towards the Royal apartments, where Louis was waiting for me.

When we arrived in front of the King's room, the doorman knocked three times, and upon Louis' answer, he entered to introduce me. As I stepped into the room, I spotted Louis wrapped in furs by the grand fireplace. He eyed me over as I approached and asked:

"Why're you wet?"

"It's of no importance. Your Highness wanted to see me?"

Louis nodded towards the doorman, giving him his leave, and now just the two of us, I adopted a less formal manner of speech.

"What did you want to speak with me about?"

"I've thought it over."

I kept silent.

"As we now speak, the documents are being prepared for de Bourgogne's release."

I let out a gust of air, feeling relieved and yet suddenly nervous.

"I thank you, brother."

"Yes, yes, well, there is a price. I want a part of your revenue on Franche Comté."

"Well, we'll negotiate for that..."

Before Louis could exclaim and demand to know how I could be so impertinent, fortunately, there came a knock on the door. The doorman entered and informed Louis, who had become a shade of purple under his rage, that Her Majesty Clementia of Hungary wished to see him.

I took the opportunity to take my leave, but then realised that Louis could rescind Jeanne's release, and so before leaving, I added an apology and another thank you.

~~~

It was some time later, while in the recreational room of the court, that I was playing a card game with some other members of the court. A messenger came up to me and whispered in my ear that Jeanne had finished her journey from the Château of Dourdan back to the royal palace, the Conciergerie. I got up, looking and talking calmly, excusing myself to the other players whom I was inconveniencing. I walked with my head tall, and to everyone around me, I was confident, and indifferent. But only I could feel my body shaking, only I could hear my heartbeat pounding. Only I could feel my exasperation at myself.

Although I felt unwell, I was happy. It seemed a strange emotion considering the situation, but I was shaking with excitement and happiness.

I reached my room and rang my bell, and my domestic took to the task of dressing me. Several hours later, once the first meeting was arranged and prepared and I was wearing my best clothes, my domestic took me to the particular room in which I would be reunited with my wife.

I knew she was already in the room, and at the thought my hands got clammy. I gulped loudly.

I spotted a domestic stifling a smile, and with the back of my hand I slapped him. I dismissed him and shook my head at how liberal servants were becoming.

I must have stayed in front of the door several minutes. I had entered a daydream, not really thinking about anything in particular. I was stirred from my thoughts when I heard a dress rustling inside the room. Someone, a woman, was pacing. I recognised Jeanne's light step. Without further hesitation, I opened the door and stepped in.

There she was, the girl who had caused so much trouble for me. She was wearing a wig, which was several shades darker than her actual hair colour. I assumed her own locks had not grown back since the trial, when her head had been shaved. She was smiling radiantly, and taking small hurried steps towards me, exclaiming how glad she was I had forgiven her. I felt a tear prickle at the corner of my eye. Looking around to dissolve the forming tear, I noticed what must have been Jeanne's domestic in a corner, and I promptly dismissed him. We were now alone in the salon.

I realised in that moment why I desperately wanted her back. I loved her. The tear formed again, and I embraced Jeanne in my arms just as the tear fell. I brushed my face against her wig and hat as I looked back down at her, and my tear had effectively been swept away. She was so small, nearly half my size.

"I have forgiven you, my sweet. But, will you forgive me? For know that I love you."

It was her turn now to cry, and she buried her head in my arms. We stayed there, in silence and I thought, *I love her*, and with a smirk she didn't see, *and Franche Comté is a bonus too*.

The room around me turned and turned and it dissolved into brighter colours, spiraling out. I felt tugged and the reds and blues and yellows called out to me, beckoning me to them. I was sucked in and I was falling yet floating at the same time. I could feel myself dissolving into a million particles, and just before I felt the last particle leave me, they all rushed back into their respective places. What was happening to me?

11

Epilogue

The colours slowly dissipated. Steam rose in front of my eyes and I was suddenly hit by pouring water. The water was too hot to be rain. I looked up, but only received soapy suds. I washed out my red eyes and slowly recognised my own shower. I quickly closed the tap, and grabbing a fluffy towel from the top left cabinet, where they always were, I wrapped it around myself. I was still dripping wet, my clinging hair making me cold. I ran through the hallway and up those familiar steps. I stepped into my lab and saw yellow liquid in a beaker, ready for use. I shivered violently and went back to the bathroom to grab a sweater which I carelessly put on. I got into a pair of jeans and went back to examine the liquid, along with my notes. The experiment wasn't finished. Tina came purring and rubbed her body against my legs. I gently shoved her away, and she stalked away in a mood. I stopped in my tracks, having a sense of déjà-vu. I glanced at the computer screen on the desk and saw the date on which I had managed to create the yellow suspension that made breaking down molecules possible. I grabbed a beaker and tried to carefully add a single drop of its contents to my solution. My sister appeared with her "BOO!", but I was prepared, and a far less amount of liquid flowed into my creation.

65 years later:

A computer screen displayed a text document entitled 'My adventure'. The hunched body over the keys didn't stir. The entire house was silent, the only noise being a song bird outside. Suddenly, a loud car broke the silence, and a key was heard. Steps up the stairs. A door opening. A scream. The body was later hauled away by a mortuary officer, laying it on a black, depressing stretcher.

"Ma'am, mind if I ask your relationship with the deceased?"

"I... I am her daughter. Or, I should use the past tense now, shouldn't I?" The woman broke into sobs. The death was not completely unexpected, but death always comes as a surprise. The previously sick grandmother was cremated within the week and her belongings dispersed amongst her next of kin, as according to her will. She had passed quietly, and almost without pain. Her grandson, a ten year old passionate for science, received her notebooks. He started reading them, beginning with the account of an experiment. However, the woman had never been able to reproduce it, and so, to avoid the psychiatric help, she had kept quiet.

Years later, her grandson is presented with a Nobel prize for advanced, turn of the century technology capable of time travelling. Every night, he talks to his grandmother, who now rests in an urn, thanking her, and telling her about his day. Even to this day, the Nobel trophy is in its rightful place, next to the original time-traveller, along with a framed photo of her in her glory days. On the shelves in every bookstore can be found a copy of My Adventure, published posthumously by her grandson. It holds the bestseller status two years in a row.

THE END

About the Author

F.J. Savina was born in France on the 29th of February 1996, but moved to Ireland with her family at the age of four. This enabled her to become fluent in both English and French. She went to an all-girls school in Dublin, but in the beginning of the second year of secondary school, she dropped out to be home-schooled. The school's teaching methods did not suit her, and so she opted out for a more suitable education. She is tutored by her parents, but her home education mostly comprises of self-learning. She enjoys a great many things, which include but are not limited to movies, reading, writing, photography, traveling, and she aspires to become someone professionally creative.

Acknowledgments

First and foremost I would like to thank Dr. Sylvie Thouësny, my editor and the instigator of this book, as well as Nicolas Fénix for the charming illustrations, and Raphaël Savina for the cover design.

I'd also like to thank the Internet, without whom this book could not boast historical accurism.

It allowed me to become real people such as chapter four's Kitty Marion, chapter eight's Marguerite David, chapter nine's Catherine of Aragon, and chapter ten's Philip V, but it also allowed me to create new characters in precise historical environments.

I give special mentions to my family and Kitty.

Thank you.

F.J. Savina